WHERE you've Got to BE

CAROLINE GERTLER

WHERE YOU'VE GOT TO BE

 Greenwillow Books

An Imprint of HarperCollinsPublishers

Where You've Got to Be
Copyright © 2022 by Caroline Gertler
All rights reserved. No part of this book may be used or reproduced in any manner whatsoever without written permission except in the case of brief quotations embodied in critical articles and reviews. Printed in the United States of America. For information address HarperCollins Children's Books, a division of HarperCollins Publishers, 195 Broadway, New York, NY 10007.
www.harpercollinschildrens.com
The text of this book is set in Matt Antique BT. Book design by Sylvie Le Floc'h

Library of Congress Cataloging-in-Publication Data

Names: Gertler, Caroline, author.
Title: Where you've got to be / Caroline Gertler.
Other titles: Where you have got to be
Description: First edition. | New York : Greenwillow Books, an Imprint of HarperCollins Publishers, [2022] | Audience: Ages 8–12. | Audience: Grades 4–6. | Summary: "Eleven-year-old Nolie navigates the challenges of sixth grade and a popular older sister"— Provided by publisher.
Identifiers: LCCN 2022006604 (print) | LCCN 2022006605 (ebook) | ISBN 9780063027053 (hardcover) | ISBN 9780063027077 (ebook)
Subjects: CYAC: Middle schools—Fiction. | Schools—Fiction. | Sisters—Fiction. | Jews—United States—Fiction. | LCGFT: Fiction.
Classification: LCC PZ7.1.G47487 Wh 2022 (print) | LCC PZ7.1.G47487 (ebook) | DDC [Fic]—dc23
LC record available at https://lccn.loc.gov/2022006604
LC ebook record available at https://lccn.loc.gov/2022006605

22 23 24 25 26 PC/LSCH 10 9 8 7 6 5 4 3 2 1   First Edition

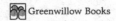 Greenwillow Books

For grandmas and sisters,
especially mine

WHeRe you've Got to Be

1

HIDDEN TREASURE

None of it would've happened if Linden hadn't ruined Nolie's summer before sixth grade.

They were supposed to spend the last days of August at Grandma's beach cottage with their cousins. Like they always did. Cousins Week was the best week of Nolie's summer. Mom and Dad and Aunt Eve and Uncle Matt went home, leaving the cousins with Grandma for a week of wave jumping and mini golf, hot dogs burned over bonfires, fresh lemonade and soft-serve ice cream that dripped sticky down your hands and wrists.

But one night over dinner while all the parents

were still there, Linden changed everything. "There's this audition workshop that would be really good for me to attend," she said.

Good for me. It was always about what was good for Linden. Apparently, this summer, it was good for Linden to end Cousins Week three days early. Like it was up to Linden to decide for Nolie—for *all* of them—what was best.

"Is it necessary?" Dad asked.

"Yes," Linden said, quietly but firmly.

She didn't have to explain. Practically the whole world knew she wanted to be a professional ballerina. She'd danced in *The Nutcracker* at Lincoln Center for the past three years. Now that she was twelve, it was her last chance to get the starring child role: Marie. She was determined to get it. Even if that meant ruining Cousins Week for everyone else.

"If it's really important, I can bring you all home early," Grandma said.

"That works for us, too," Aunt Eve said, like turning Cousins Week into Cousins Half-Week was no big deal. "Give the kids more time to settle in before school starts."

"No fair!" Nolie piped up, her voice shrill and babyish. She was eleven, only fourteen months younger than Linden, but sometimes, she felt like there were years, not months, between them. Somehow, Linden being older meant that she always got her way. There's no chance their cousins would stand for this. "C'mon, don't you guys want to stay the whole time?"

Anna, who was thirteen, and a competitive horseback rider, shrugged, and tossed the long tail of her braid over her shoulder. "I could use more time to train at the stables."

Nolie looked to the twins, Gabe and Eli, who were eight and practically clueless. They worked at their corncobs like a pair of puppies gnawing bones.

"There goes my week of kid-free rest and relaxation," Uncle Matt said, trying to be funny.

But it wasn't funny. Not to Nolie.

"Please, Mom?" Nolie knew she sounded whiny. She could see it in the irritated expression on Mom's face, the way her eyebrows pinched together in a deep V. "Can't I stay with Grandma, alone?"

But Mom shook her head, not considering that option. No one did.

No one took Nolie's side.

Not even Grandma, whose face flashed a quick flicker of disappointment as the grown-up talk turned to logistics.

Only Nolie felt a seething, twisting ember of anger spark inside her. A fury of injustice. Her sister had ruined Cousins Week before it even began.

Just like Linden had ruined everything lately. Last time Mom set up an ice cream sundae bar for dessert, Linden rolled her eyes, grabbed a few mini marshmallows, and went back to her phone. Or when Dad offered to take them to an amusement park, Linden said the rides made her nauseated.

It was like ever since Linden had turned twelve in April, a switch had flipped in her, and her mood was more often "off" than "on." She ignored Nolie most of the time, glued to her phone, watching stupid dance videos, or learning how to braid her hair into more and more elaborate styles. Fish tail, French, Dutch . . . you name it. Linden used to beg to practice on Nolie's hair. But recently, when Nolie offered to let her, Linden scowled and said, "Meh. Your hair's too thin." Sometimes, that summer, it felt like there was a stranger sleeping in the bed across from Nolie. Not her sister.

Now, Nolie'd had enough. She couldn't snap out of her sour, angry mood for the four days of Cousins Week that they did have. Not that anyone cared how she felt. Linden and Anna carried on as usual, leading the charge into the ocean, directing them on how to build a giant moat in the sand, deciding when it was time for a break. Nolie's grumpiness only meant that she got left behind. Last one into the ocean, last to pick her ball color in mini golf, last to take a shower so the water was barely warm for her turn.

Grandma, at least, showed some sympathy, even if she didn't outright say that she was disappointed, too. She asked Nolie if she had any special dinner requests, and didn't even sigh when Nolie asked for her favorite lemon-parmesan risotto, which meant Grandma spending nearly an hour stirring a pot of rice over the hot stove. She let Nolie have everyone's favorite piece—the dog—for their game of Monopoly.

Grandma even gave Nolie the first choice of treasure. Every year at the end of Cousins Week, she gave the grandchildren a treasure from the beach to take home: a piece of green or blue sea glass, an interesting shell, a tiny bottle filled with sand.

Now Grandma held open her straw beach bag and pulled out a smaller plastic bag with something that clinked inside.

Nolie peeked in to discover a jumble of seashell necklaces. "Oh, these are so pretty!" She couldn't help but feel uplifted by the necklaces. By choosing one—on the lime green cord—and letting Grandma slip it around her neck. A treasure to wear all the time, that she could reach up and touch whenever she wanted to be reminded of their beach days.

It was like her best friend, Jessa. She had an amethyst crystal necklace that her grandmother had given to her before she died, for good luck. Now she'd have a special necklace of her own, too.

"Thank you." Nolie threw her arms around Grandma, inhaling her soapy, floral scent.

Grandma pulled her into a tight hug on her lap. "Mmm, I need to savor you," she said, resting her cheek against Nolie's head. "Next year you might be too big for me to hold this way."

Nolie thought she was already too big, but she

didn't say it. She let Grandma hold her as long as she wanted. She didn't want any of it to end.

At least back in the city, they lived close enough to Grandma that they saw her almost every week. Unlike the cousins, who mostly came in from New Jersey for holidays: Rosh Hashanah and Yom Kippur, Thanksgiving, Passover. And Jessa would be back from visiting her father in LA by now.

On the last day, the rain fell all morning. When it stopped and the sun peeked out, Nolie took a break from packing to get in her last breaths of beach air. As she walked down to the beach, she spotted one of Grandma's seashell necklaces on the side of the deck. The cord was aqua blue—Linden's. She must've dropped it by accident.

Nolie picked it up to return to her, but Linden took it with a muttered "thanks" and no expression of relief. She didn't immediately slip it over her head, like Nolie would've done if that'd happened to her. Maybe she was being cold to Nolie, to get back at her for how bratty she'd been acting the last few days.

Later, as Nolie threw some scrap papers into the trash, something blue caught her eye. Aqua blue.

There was nothing gross or wet in that trash. Nolie couldn't help but reach her hand in to pull it out.

Linden's shell necklace. Again.

Linden was trying to get rid of it. But Nolie wouldn't let her.

What if Linden regretted throwing out Grandma's treasure when they got home? Then she'd be grateful that Nolie'd saved it for her.

On the train ride to the city, all the cousins wore their necklaces. Nolie liked how it connected them. Except for Linden.

Even Grandma noticed. "Linden, where's yours?" she asked.

Linden reached her hand to her neck and smiled. "I packed it with my stuff."

The lie rolled off her tongue.

Nolie narrowed her eyes at Linden. But Linden was looking everywhere—out the window, at Anna's laughing face telling a story, at the twins poking each other—except at Nolie.

Linden's seashell necklace was, in fact, tucked in the folds of Nolie's underwear, for protection, in a side pocket of her suitcase.

Granted, the underwear was clean, because she'd brought enough for a week, but still.

It gave Nolie a gleam of satisfaction, like somehow she was getting back at Linden for ruining Cousins Week, by packing the necklace with her underwear.

Uncle Matt picked up Anna, Eli, and Gabe by the ticket booth in Penn Station. Grandma hailed a taxi to drop off Nolie and Linden at their apartment building on West Eighty-ninth Street. The contrast between the utter calm of the beach cottage with its creaky screen windows and salty fresh air, and the sticky, cracked seats of the taxicab that smelled of the hot dog with sauerkraut that the driver was eating, made Nolie even more miserable to be back in the city.

"Bye, Grandma. Love you, see you soon," each sister said, giving her a hug as they got out of the cab.

"Love you more, see you soonest," Grandma said in return, like always, before the taxi pulled away.

But the minute Nolie and Linden were alone on the sidewalk in front of their building, they were all silence.

Linden slung her bag over her shoulder and

marched in the front door ahead of Nolie. She didn't even say hello to José, the doorman who held the door open for them.

"Hi," Nolie said in an apologetic voice to make up for Linden's rudeness.

"Welcome back, young ladies," José said.

Linden jabbed the elevator button with her finger.

"Why are you mad at me?" Nolie asked, shivering in the lobby air-conditioning that blew a million times colder than the ceiling fans at the beach cottage.

"Because you're such a pain. You made the week so miserable with your attitude," Linden said.

"*Me?*" Nolie tried to keep her voice quiet, so José wouldn't overhear their argument. "First of all, it wasn't even a week, because *you* cut it short."

The elevator doors opened, letting out an elderly woman who lived on a floor above them, walking her three cranky Chihuahuas.

"The problem is," Linden started as soon as the elevator doors closed them inside, "you wouldn't understand. It's not like you *do* anything. Besides sit around and read and pick your nails or whatever. You don't get what it's like to have a passion. Something that's more important to you than anything."

Nolie couldn't argue with that. It was true—she didn't have a *thing*, like Linden with ballet. Instead, she tried lots of different things. Whatever sparked her interest at the moment: gymnastics, figure skating, ceramics, theater, flute, and cello. You name it, Nolie had tried it. But really, she was happiest simply *being*. She couldn't imagine having one main activity that she did for hours and hours a day.

Still, having a passion, like ballet for Linden, shouldn't mean that it was more important than everything else. Than your sister, or your whole family.

"You ruined the week," Nolie said as the elevator doors opened on their landing. "Like you ruin everything." With those words, the ember of anger flared brighter. She couldn't stop herself. "You even threw out Grandma's necklace!"

Linden lunged for her. But before Linden could grab her and twist her arm or pull her hair, Nolie darted down the hall to push through their unlocked front door and into their apartment, to the safety of Mom and Dad, who were waiting with freshly baked lasagna for dinner.

Their parents bombarded them with questions about what they'd done and how much fun they'd had, as if they'd been away all summer. Not just four days.

But Cousins Week was supposed to be seven days, and every single one of those days mattered to Nolie. She'd wake up early in the morning, and stay up late at night until her eyes closed against her will, to make the days stretch out forever and ever. Linden had taken away three whole days from the week she looked forward to all year.

Over dinner, Linden cut up her lasagna into tiny, neat squares. She wiped sauce and grease off her chin in between each bite and made plans to get to the ballet studio early tomorrow morning, like nothing was wrong. Like they shouldn't still be eating burgers fresh off the grill on Grandma's deck, the seagulls squawking overhead, the constant waves lulling them to peace. Instead of in their dark, cramped apartment, where you had no idea whether there was a beautiful August sunset because it might as well be winter.

Not to mention that Linden sounded just like the adults when she discussed her plans. She didn't chatter on and on about how excited she was for the workshop, like she would've done before. She didn't get up from the table in the middle of the meal to show them how high she could lift and turn out her leg, like she used to do. Nolie felt like the only kid sitting at the grown-ups table.

All Nolie had to hold on to was the seashell that hung around her neck. And even that was now a reminder of what she was missing, of Grandma and the beach. And, of what Linden had tried to throw away.

That night, while Linden was showering, Nolie looked around their room for a place to keep Linden's seashell necklace.

Their shared bedroom was tiny. Twin beds took up the walls along the sides of the room, solid wood headboards pushed against the window. At the feet of their beds, they each had a small desk and dresser. With all that furniture squeezed in, there was barely any space left to move around, let alone breathe.

Mom had a rule that if one of them needed privacy, she had to ask her sister politely and they both had to agree. No surprise, it always ended up being Linden who wanted privacy. Because Linden took up more space, with her ballet stuff overflowing her dresser. Stacks of leotards, tights, leg warmers, filmy skirts. Ballet slippers and pointe shoes, ribbons and threads and needles, bobby pins and hair spray. Every morning she'd pack those things in the black ballet duffel their parents got her for Hanukkah the year she was nine and Nolie was eight. The first year that Linden danced in *The Nutcracker*, as an angel. Monogrammed in pink cursive on one side: *Linden*, above an embroidered pair of ballet slippers tied with a ribbon.

Nolie'd cried with jealous rage when Linden opened that gift on the first night of Hanukkah. She kicked the special box set of Ramona books that she'd unwrapped across the room. The books slid out of the case, across the floor, with a shocking clatter.

Instead of a special monogrammed duffel for her passion, all Nolie had was a Walgreens paper bag packed with stuff from every activity she'd tried but hadn't stuck with: a leotard, a sketchbook and paint set, a tennis racket with a broken string, a recorder, a chessboard minus a few pieces. That bag lived in the back of the closet, behind where their school uniform kilts hung.

Nolie considered putting Linden's seashell necklace in that bag of stuff in the closet or in the jumbled mess of her desk drawer, but it might get broken.

If she put it in her usual spot, on the shelf above her desk, along with her other Cousins Week treasures, Linden would see it. Linden hadn't wanted the necklace, but if she found out Nolie had taken it, she'd be indignant. It'd be just another thing to drive her away. Another reason for her to be annoyed with Nolie.

Maybe Nolie shouldn't have taken it. Yet now that she had, she couldn't bring herself to throw it out. Or to give it back. She needed to put it in a place where no one would look.

She sunk down on her bed to survey their room.

And then it occurred to her: the one spot she couldn't see from where she was sitting was *behind* the bed. On the dusty windowsill, in the space behind the headboard, where no one ever cleaned.

The perfect hiding spot.

2
WHAT'S IN A NAME

Things only got worse the last week of summer break.

Jessa texted that she was spending extra time in LA to finish a theater program, which made the week stretch out endlessly for Nolie.

Nothing captured her interest—none of the books she borrowed from the library, or the TV shows she streamed. She started to make chocolate chip cookies and then realized they were out of chips. She baked them plain, but they just weren't the same without the bursts of chocolate. A few times she went to Dad's shoe store, Joey's, to help. But mostly, she was bored.

And then, class lists arrived. Nolie opened up the

email and immediately scanned for her name where she expected it to be, right below Jessa's: *Jessamine Baker, Magnolia Beck.* Where her name always was, since they'd become best friends in second grade. They'd been in the same class every year since.

But now, Nolie's name was listed in Ms. Vazquez's homeroom. And there was another name above Nolie's: Serena Alderson. Shady Serena!

Nolie found Jessa's name on Mr. Fink's homcroom list. With Calliope, the new girl Jessa'd started becoming friends with last year.

Help! Nolie texted Jessa. *Different classes!!! What?!?*

Jessa's bubble of typing dots appeared and disappeared and reappeared again.

Nolie held her breath waiting for the reply. In Nolie's opinion, there was only one word for her and Jessa not being together: *disaster*! Or two words—for emphasis: *total disaster*!

Jessa's final reply wasn't exactly what Nolie'd expected: an emoji. One of those worried smiley faces that meant "eek!"

Nolie sent back a vomit emoji. Even though, for her, an emoji could hardly capture the devastation.

Nolie'd been one of the shyest girls in the grade the first few years of school. She had this thing where she assumed she was invisible. Everyone always noticed Linden first. "Oh, you're Linden's little sister," they'd say, after making the connection. Even though Nolie wasn't so much littler. In fact, she was almost as tall as Linden, and she wore a size bigger in clothes. But Linden was the memorable one. The ballerina, the star.

Things changed when Jessa, who was always loud and funny and chatty, declared Nolie her best friend in second grade. All Nolie had to do was stick to Jessa. Being with Jessa made Nolie feel bold and strong and funny. She made Nolie feel seen.

The day before the first day of sixth grade, Jessa was finally home. She invited Nolie over to hang out.

Nolie woke up late. She rushed to throw on clothes—yesterday's jean shorts and a tie-dye T-shirt they'd made for field day at the end of fifth grade— and pulled her hair into a messy ponytail. She slipped Grandma's seashell necklace, which she was excited to show Jessa, around her neck.

She couldn't wait to see Jessa, yet she felt oddly

nervous the whole way over on the crosstown bus to her apartment on the East Side. Her nerves would settle as soon as she saw her best friend.

But when Jessa answered the door, Nolie drew back in surprise. Jessa was different. It was like everything about her had grown, in every direction. She clearly needed a bra, and her sandy brown hair, parted down the middle, hung longer down her back and was streaked with blond. Maybe from salon highlights, or from the California sun. Even her face seemed longer, her chin sharper. Only her expression was less animated than usual. Maybe it was her makeup—too much black eyeliner and mascara, and a pale pink lip gloss. Like a preteen celebrity had abducted Jessa and put this girl in her place.

"What's wrong?" Nolie asked. Not how she'd planned to greet her best friend for the first time in almost three months.

"Not much. Just tired." Jessa yawned, stretching her arms over her head to show off her tanned, flat stomach beneath her crop top. "I was up way too late last night."

As she followed Jessa down the hall to her room,

Nolie wondered what she'd been doing up so late. Because Jessa must've been chatting or texting with someone. And it hadn't been Nolie.

Jessa was an only child, with a whole big bedroom to herself. Her favorite color, lavender, was immediately evident from the lavender walls of her room and the lavender flower print on the shades and lavender easy chair in the corner. She'd stuck with lavender ever since third grade, when she'd switched from orange. And she didn't just switch her favorite from orange to lavender—she now absolutely despised orange. Jessa had very definite opinions about things.

Nolie wondered if Jessa still loved lavender, or if she'd decided that was babyish over the summer. Because today, she was wearing a gray crop top over black denim cutoffs. The only lavender was in her amethyst necklace—the one from her grandmother. At least Jessa hadn't outgrown that.

Nolie didn't even have a favorite color. Sometimes it was teal. Or mauve. Or lemon yellow, or maybe minty green, if she was forced to choose. Maybe she'd never gotten the chance to pick a favorite color, because she didn't have a room of her own to decorate. But the truth was, Nolie liked lots of colors. She didn't get why people always wanted to know your favorite.

Jessa propped herself against the jumble of pillows at the head of her queen-sized bed, wrapping her arms around a sequined rainbow pillow with a winking face. Nolie curled into the faux fur beanbag chair on the floor. It was soothing to rub her palms against the fur, pushing it up first in one direction and then patting it down the other.

"How was Cousins Week?" Jessa asked.

"Linden ruined it. We had to come back early for some ballet thing." Nolie knew that even though being an only child meant Jessa pretty much got everything she wanted, Jessa envied her for having a sister and cousins that she was close to. Last summer, before fifth grade, Jessa had come to spend a weekend at Grandma's beach cottage, but Nolie'd made it clear that she couldn't stay for Cousins Week. Jessa had asked why not, like she truly didn't get that Cousins Week was special, just for cousins. Maybe that had hurt Jessa more than Nolie'd realized. Now she didn't even have to downplay the fun of Cousins Week for Jessa, because it truly hadn't been fun.

"That sucks," Jessa said. "LA was actually better than ever this year."

"You had fun with your dad?" Jessa's parents were divorced, and her dad produced reality TV shows in Hollywood. She always bragged about how she had the best time when she visited him.

But this time, instead of bragging about seeing this and that celebrity and the restaurants they ate at and the cool rides at Disneyland, Jessa sighed. Cringed, almost. "Yeah, he was okay. But the TV business, it's not for me. This new theater camp I went to, though, was amazing. I loved being onstage, doing live theater. That's what I want to be. A serious actor."

"Wow," Nolie said. "Sounds like you've found your thing. Like Linden."

"Yeah. Like that." Jessa nodded. "I've really got to focus this year. So I get a good role in the middle school play."

"How about the fall musical?" Nolie asked. Every year the middle school did a fall musical and a spring play. Nolie wasn't a particularly talented singer, but she'd thought it could be fun to try out for the musical this year.

"Depends on what it is," Jessa said. "Some musicals are too silly for me."

"You're going to be so busy," Nolie said. She felt herself wanting to pick at a patch of dry skin on her thumb, so she pulled at the fur on the beanbag instead. "I hope we get to hang out even though we're in different homerooms."

Jessa flicked her wrist, brushing off Nolie's worries. "It doesn't matter *that* much, the way our schedules work. I think we have some classes together, like chorus and PE. You selected chorus instead of instruments, right?"

"Yeah," Nolie said. Of course she'd selected chorus. They'd been required to pick an instrument in fourth grade, so she'd chosen violin. But after two years, her playing still sounded like a screeching owl and drove everyone at home crazy. Even though her singing voice wasn't much better than her violin playing, now that they got to choose to drop instruments for chorus, it was a no-brainer.

So sure, she'd have chorus and PE with Jessa. But

she knew that Calliope was also in chorus, and in Jessa's homeroom, and the whole grade had PE at the same time, so those two would be together practically all day. Not to mention that Calliope and Jessa even spent Sundays together: they went to the same church and Sunday school.

"And we'll see each other at lunch," Jessa said, noticing that Nolie was being quiet.

"You'll save me a seat, right?" Nolie asked, her throat tight. *Seeing* Jessa at lunch wasn't the same as *sitting* with her.

Jessa fidgeted with the amethyst crystal around her neck.

"Oh, look! My grandmother gave me a necklace, too!" Nolie held out the seashell, which had gotten tucked under her T-shirt, for Jessa to admire.

Instead, Jessa's mouth fell open and she hugged her rainbow pillow protectively against her. "You're lucky your grandma's still alive. You don't have to rub it in my face."

That's not what Nolie'd meant. But before she could answer, Jessa's mom, Andie, flung open the door. Jessa glared.

"Nolie!" Andie seemed happier to see Nolie than Jessa had. Jessa's expression turned even more sour. "Happy almost start of school!" Andie said, ignoring Jessa. Andie, at least, looked the same as always. Her cheeks had a healthy glow, and her curly blond hair was darker at the roots, still wet from a shower. She'd probably just come back from a run around the loop in Central Park.

Nolie smiled and gave a shy wave. Jessa's mom was so different from Nolie's mom, it took her a little while to get used to Andie again at the beginning of each school year. She'd always been the dream mom that Nolie wished she had. Well, sort of. Unlike Nolie's parents, Andie didn't have to work. Instead, Andie was there—all the time—to make sure that Jessa's life was better and easier. One time she'd taken them home for a playdate and Jessa complained that Andie hadn't restocked the pantry with her favorite cookies. Andie teased, "You know, my only purpose on this earth is to take care of you! That's all I do with my life!"

Nolie didn't get the joke, because to her, it did seem like that's all Andie did. Aside from running or having coffee with the other moms who didn't have to work. Everything else Andie made time for was related to Jessa and their school, like volunteering to be a class rep and host holiday festivals and end-of-year celebrations. Things that Nolie's mom never signed up for because she was too busy.

"How was your summer?" Andie ran her fingers through her wet curls, which sproinged back into place. Nolie wished her hair bounced like that and didn't just hang dully in its usual ponytail.

"It was good," Nolie said.

Andie hesitated, as if she wanted to ask follow-up questions, to get more specific, but Jessa looked daggers at her, and she took the hint.

"Okay, well, so great to see you again, hon. And when your other friend gets here, we'll have lunch." She left without shutting the door.

"Close the door, Mom!" Jessa shouted from her throne-like perch.

"Your other friend?" Nolie was confused. Jessa hadn't mentioned inviting anyone else.

"Yeah, I invited Calliope. To make it more celebratory. You know." Jessa didn't meet Nolie's eyes as she spoke.

Nolie most certainly didn't know. If anything, having Calliope there would make it more awkward. For Nolie, at least.

The intercom buzzed, announcing that Calliope had arrived.

"C'mon." Jessa jumped up from her bed, with her usual animated face again.

Nolie almost held her back, for one last moment of assurance. She hadn't answered Nolie's question, hadn't promised to save her a seat at lunch. But Nolie didn't want to seem overly needy. Of course Jessa would save a seat for her. Why wouldn't she? It's not like they'd gotten into a fight or anything.

Calliope entered in a rush of giggles and hugs, her face extra tan and sparkling with pink blush. "Look what I did!" she said to Jessa, tucking her streaky blond hair behind her ear to show off a tiny gold star above the hoop in her original piercing. The flesh of her ear looked red.

"You did it?" Jessa squealed. "But last night you said your mom—"

"I know! But this morning I convinced her. I promised to babysit my siblings this weekend!"

"Lucky!" Jessa said. "Mom, can I get a second piercing, too, if I babysit with her?"

Andie shook her head and smiled.

Nolie touched her hand to her own ear, which had no piercings. Not because her mom wouldn't let her. It just hadn't been something she'd been interested in doing. Not yet.

The lunch was total Andie-and-Jessa overkill. The small dining table in the family room was set with a white tablecloth and silver-rimmed china plates and crystal glasses. Andie made crustless turkey and cucumber tea sandwiches, and lemonade she'd probably squeezed herself. There was a tower of sugar cookies that Andie and Jessa had baked and decorated, cut out with a number six shape and frosted in the school colors, blue and burgundy.

If it was lunch at Nolie's house, her mom probably wouldn't even be there to help host. Instead, Nolie would make a box of mac 'n' cheese and pass around a carton of Oreos. But this was Jessa's.

Andie went into the kitchen to do some washing up as the girls took their seats at the table. And there was the finishing touch: at each place, a brand-new canvas pencil pouch, personalized in rainbow embroidery with their names. Calliope, Jessa, and . . . Magnolia.

"Is this mine?" Nolie asked, lifting it up to look closer.

"Is there another Magnolia here?" Jessa asked. Calliope laughed. "Seriously, I thought maybe this year, we could call you Magnolia. It's such a pretty name." She looked directly at Nolie then, her brown eyes wide and innocent.

"Yeah," Calliope chimed in. "It sounds so mysterious and majestic."

"Magnificent," Jessa said. "All those spicy *m* words. Magnificent Magnolia." They laughed. Nolie didn't think they meant to laugh *at* her, but it sure felt like it.

"Nobody calls me Magnolia," Nolie said.

It's not that Nolie hated her real name. Not at all. It simply wasn't *her*. Magnolia sounded like a precious girl from the South with golden blond ringlets. It didn't suit her: brown-haired, Jewish, New York City born and bred. The only people who called her Magnolia were substitute teachers or doctors or other people who didn't know she went by Nolie. Whenever there was an option on a form to specify the name you'd like to be called, Mom always put down *Nolie*.

"Let's try it. Magnolia."

"Why, Jessamine?" Nolie threw back at her. Jessa actually did hate her full name. Nolie knew that. But she couldn't help it. Her throat felt scratchy, and she took a few sips of her lemonade.

Jessa's acting skills had improved; she looked like she might actually cry. "You know that's totally different," she said. She explained to Calliope, "My dad insisted on making my full name Jessamine instead of Jessica, which my mom wanted, so the name Jessamine is a constant reminder to her. A slap in the face, she calls it."

Calliope shrugged. "People used to call me Callie. But I'm so glad I'm Calliope now. It's like I've become the person I was always meant to be." She framed her face with her hands in a movie-star pose.

Nolie considered. Was Magnolia the person *she* was always meant to be? If she started going by Magnolia, would it make her different? Did she even want to be different, anyway?

The pencil pouches were super cute, with their names spelled out in rainbow cursive letters and a heart at the end. Nolie knew Jessa and Calliope would use theirs every day. She could already see how they'd pull the pouches out of their backpacks in class and set them on their desks. A symbol of their bond, that they belonged together.

If Nolie didn't use hers because it said Magnolia instead of Nolie, she'd be sabotaging herself. Making herself feel left out, over something as trivial as a name.

"Let's just try it." Jessa flashed her wide, straight-teeth smile. No braces. She'd gotten them off before she left for LA. "Magnolia."

Calliope giggled. Even Jessa struggled to keep a straight face. Nolie sort of pretended to giggle, too. To laugh at herself along with them. But it came out sounding more like a frog's croak. She cringed and drank down the last drops of her lemonade.

"More lemonade?" Andie called from the kitchen. Nolie's glass was empty and her throat dry. She wanted more. But she didn't want to speak; her throat felt all croaky. She waited a moment for Andie to come out with the pitcher to refill their glasses, but she didn't.

So Nolie pushed back her chair to get up from the table, to bring her glass to the kitchen for more. But when she stood up, the tablecloth had gotten stuck to her legs somehow and she started dragging it with her. In her attempt to keep from pulling everything off the table, she knocked over the chair behind her.

"Oh, shoot!" Nolie cried out, dropping her glass on the floor. Thankfully, the carpet was soft and nothing broke. And it was already empty except for a couple of ice cubes that she quickly scooped back in. She picked up the glass and the chair and let out a deep breath.

Jessa and Calliope stared at Nolie like she was a clumsy alien who'd crash-landed her UFO on their happy tea party.

"You okay, Magnolia?" Jessa narrowed her eyes, like she was checking Nolie for symptoms.

And then Nolie did feel flushed and hot. Maybe— *please please please*—she *was* coming down with a fever. And that's why she was acting so weird. Not because there was something awkward about her. Not the way she saw herself reflected on Jessa's and Calliope's faces.

"I'm fine," Nolie said. "I just—I kind of have a headache. And I promised Dad I'd help him at the store this afternoon. Back to school shopping and all."

"Okay, got it," Jessa said. Not a word of protest. No begging Nolie to stay longer.

Nolie brought her glass to the kitchen. She said thank you and good-bye to Andie, who was taken aback to see her leave so suddenly.

"Don't forget your pouch!" Andie came running with it to the front door and held it out to Nolie.

"Thanks," Nolie mumbled. She looked down at the pouch—at *Magnolia* embroidered in rainbow letters. The name smiled up at her, bright and cheerful. She pinched the edge of the pouch in her fingers, like she was picking up a piece of litter, and tucked it under her arm.

Andie must've sensed what Nolie was feeling. She pulled Nolie into a hug, holding on a few extra beats, as if she knew this might be the last time she'd get to say good-bye to her. That it might be the last time Jessa invited her over.

It sure felt that way to Nolie.

3
JOEY'S SHOES

Nolie walked and walked and walked after leaving Jessa's. She walked until she got to Fifth Avenue, along Central Park, and there was no crosstown bus in sight. The sticky heat made her sweat and her T-shirt clung to her back, but she decided to keep walking, through the park to the West Side.

It was always cooler in the park, where the trees provided shelter from the sun. Little kids raced by on their scooters, dogs paraded around the Great Lawn, and Nolie bought a lemon ice from a vendor.

Just being in the park made her feel better. But as she got closer to home, she realized no one would be there. If her mom was like Andie, she'd be at home, ready to do something to make Nolie feel better, like take her for a milkshake. But Mom had taken the day off work to bring Linden to Capezio to fit her pointe shoes and buy her new leotards and tights and all the other ballet things that cost a lot more money than Mom and Dad wanted to spend.

Dad was at Joey's, the shoe store he owned. Nolie hadn't really promised to help him that day, but it was better than being home alone.

Joey's Shoes was on a stretch of Broadway across from the movie theater and the Shooting Star diner, between a pharmacy that had been there as long as Joey's and a new bakery that specialized in bite-sized cupcakes in all kinds of wacky flavors like rainbow tie-dye and chocolate-chip pancake. The sidewalk was crowded with vendors selling fruit from wooden crates and bags displayed on drop cloths. On the corner was a newsstand where Ahmed sat on a stool behind a plastic window. Nolie sometimes bought packs of pink Trident or plain M&Ms from him.

The bell above the door jingled as Nolie pushed it open. The air-conditioning greeted her with a welcome blast. Dad knelt on the floor, fitting sneakers on a kid with a hovering mom. Brenda, the store manager, worked the register. She and the other salespeople welcomed Nolie with nods and smiles. Nolie was most definitely their favorite. Maybe because she was the only one who came by to help. Linden almost never came. Not since she'd gotten serious about ballet. But still. It felt nice to be appreciated.

Joey's Shoes was known for giving out balloons to the kid customers. A couple years ago, Brenda taught Nolie how to use the helium machine. When it was busy, she'd let Nolie do the balloons. And sometimes she'd ask Nolie to help with the shoe displays in the two large plate-glass windows. It was relaxing, like a logic puzzle, to think about the best way to arrange the shoes, to make passersby want to come in and shop.

Dad looked up at her and winked but stayed with his customer, a boy who was maybe six or seven, wearing basketball shorts and a faded T-shirt. That meant this mother and child were not regular customers, and maybe the mom was even giving Dad a hard time. Parents could be tough when it came to buying new shoes for their kids.

Nolie pretended to browse the fancy dress shoes on the wall opposite, to eavesdrop on what was happening.

"Are you sure these will fit him through Thanksgiving?" the mom asked, her voice tight and insistent. "The last ones you sold us, he outgrew in a month."

"Growth spurt," Dad said. "Lay off the ice cream."

The boy laughed; the mom pursed her lips.

Dad needed some help here.

Nolie turned around. The boy had on a pair of expensive-looking hightops that probably cost more than the mom had budgeted.

"Those sneakers are so cool!" Nolie said. "They look great on you!"

The mom's tense shoulders softened a bit. The boy beamed and stretched out his legs for everyone to admire the fancy sneakers.

"Let me see you walk around," the mom said.

The boy jumped up and raced around the store, swerving to avoid other customers. When he got back, Dad gave him a high-five, and the mom bent down to feel his toes.

"See," Dad said, pulling the sneakers at the heel.

"The next size up was falling off his foot."

"Shoes that are too big—that's the worst," Nolie chimed in.

"Okay, okay." The mom cracked a smile. "We'll take these. And hope they last us more than a month!"

"Can I have a balloon?" the boy asked as his mom went up to pay.

"Of course," Dad said. "My trusty assistant here can help you with that."

"What color do you want?" Nolie asked.

"Blue. No, green. No, blue," the boy said.

Nolie laughed. "How about one of each, for being such a good customer today?"

"Yay!" The boy double fist-pumped and ran up to tell his mom.

Dad went into the back office with Nolie while she fished out the balloons to inflate.

"Well done there," he said, patting her shoulder. "See, we make a great team."

"Yup." In the back of her head, Nolie had this idea that Dad hoped she'd take over the store one day. Joey's Shoes was named after Dad's grandfather, Joseph Levy, who started the store seventy-three years ago and counting. Nolie's middle name was Josephine, after him. Grandma had taken over the store from her father, and now Dad was in charge. He was always encouraging Nolie to help out whenever she showed an interest.

Dad gave her a questioning look. "Hey, weren't you supposed to be at Jessa's today?"

"I was," Nolie said. "But it kind of wrapped up early." She didn't want to get into it. She glanced at the stupid pouch she'd put down on Dad's desk in the back office so she could zap the balloons with helium. She tied them off with red strings for contrast.

"Well, happy to have you here. It's been a day." He gestured around at the mess of shoes and boxes.

The store wasn't too busy now. Midafternoon meant post-lunch hour, naptime for the little kids. Mornings through lunchtime and after school and work were busiest. But Nolie could tell it had been a whirlwind. Shoeboxes were scattered all over the cracked leather benches, which Dad said needed to be updated with new fabric one of these days. A wall of boxes was piled almost ceiling high on the checkout counter.

After giving the boy his balloons and telling him to enjoy his new sneakers, Nolie got to work putting shoes back in their boxes, making sure to match sizes and colors and right with left.

"You excited to go back to school tomorrow?" Brenda asked as they stacked up boxes on a dolly to bring down to the storeroom.

"Yeah, I guess," Nolie said.

"Stupid question, right." Brenda shook her head. "What kid is happy to go back to school?"

Nolie *would've* been happy if she was in the same homeroom as Jessa. If Jessa wasn't replacing her with Calliope. If everything was the same as it had been at the beginning of last year. But this year, so far, everything was different.

"How about Linden?" Brenda asked. "Busy as ever?"

"Oh, yeah," Nolie said. "She's in major bat mitzvah prep mode, and she wants to be Marie in *The Nutcracker* this year."

Brenda tsked in disbelief. "Our very own Linden Beck, a ballet star!"

Linden had decided to be a ballerina the very

first time Mom took them to see *The Nutcracker* at Lincoln Center. She was mesmerized, watching the girls on stage in frilly dresses, their hair curled and pulled back in stiff bows, dancing in the party scene. From that moment, she said all she wanted was to be Marie. The star. The girl who's given a toy nutcracker by her godfather, then enters a dream world and takes a magic boat to the Land of Sweets with her prince, where she sits on a throne and watches the candies and sweets dance. Now Linden did ballet six days a week and had danced roles in *The Nutcracker* every year since she was an angel at age nine. This year she didn't have even one free day; that was now filled with tutoring to prepare for her bat mitzvah in February.

Nolie, on the other hand, had to drop out of toddlers 'n' tutus because she got dizzy and fell into a heap when they did twirls. Nolie didn't mind—she didn't long to be onstage like Linden. The view of the ballet was better from the cushy velvet seats than from the stage. When you're in the middle of a scene, you don't get the whole picture like you do when you're watching from the audience. She'd have to be on the bima in front of the whole synagogue when it was her turn to get bat mitzvahed, the year after Linden, but that was just for an hour or two of one day. It was nothing like Linden, doing dozens of performances in front of three thousand people at Lincoln Center over the course of the ballet season.

"We're lucky there's one Beck kid not too busy to help," Brenda said, wiping the dust on her hands from the shoeboxes on her shirt. "Carry on the legacy, and all. You know, you remind me of Lenore in that picture of her in front of the store, from when she's about your age."

That was a real compliment. Especially coming from Brenda, who claimed to be a tough judge of character. Lenore was Grandma—Dad's mom. Daughter of Joseph, who started Joey's Shoes. Spending time at Joey's used to mean more time with Grandma, too, because she'd worked in the store every day until last year, when she finally decided to retire.

In the grainy black-and-white photograph that Brenda was talking about, Grandma was maybe eleven or twelve years old. She wore a short-sleeved blouse tucked into a skirt, her dark brown hair pulled back into barrettes at the sides. She said she already knew at that age that she wanted to run the store one day. Even though she was about the same age that Nolie was now, she must've been a million times more mature.

Nolie stayed at Joey's until closing time, to walk home with Dad. She picked up the pencil pouch while Dad packed up his briefcase, double-checked that the cash register was locked, and set the alarms.

"That new?" Dad asked, noticing the pouch for the first time.

"Jessa gave it to me. Today." She held it out for him to read the name.

"Looks a few letters too long," he said, squinting. "You want to go by Magnolia now? I'm game for it. It's a beautiful name, even if Grandma said it wasn't Jewish enough."

"She did?" That was news.

"Oops," Dad slapped his hand over his mouth. "Grandma got her influence in your middle name. I'm onboard with Magnolia."

"Please, no!" She folded the pouch in half so the name was on the inside, not visible. "Jessa made it like this."

"Ah, so *she* wants to call you Magnolia? Or the bag people made an error? Maybe she can get you a new one?"

"Da-ad. Enough," Nolie groaned.

A name printed on a bag seemed like such a trivial thing. Especially with all the homeless people they passed on the walk up Broadway back to their apartment. People had much bigger problems in the world than a personalized pencil pouch that wasn't quite right.

Did names matter so much, anyway? Sure, they defined how people thought of you. She knew how much Grandma loved her. She secretly thought she was Grandma's favorite, even if Grandma would never actually say it. But would Grandma love her as much if she went by Magnolia, a name she didn't like, instead of by Nolie? And would going by Magnolia make Jessa like her more?

Not that she even had to make a choice. People could call her whatever they wanted to. That's how she'd gotten to be called Nolie, in the first place. When Nolie was a baby, Linden was just starting to speak and couldn't pronounce her full name, so she'd been the one to call her that, and it'd stuck.

Maybe names didn't matter that much. Maybe a name was just a name. Like any other words, names didn't really mean anything about who you were on the inside.

On their way home, Dad got a text from Mom that Linden was famished and they decided to stop for a quick dinner at the Shooting Star diner.

Good for them, Nolie thought, feeling a pang of irritation that they didn't invite her. On the plus side, she got a little time home alone while they were still out. In their tiny room that was half the size of Jessa's. No queen-sized beds for them.

Even better, Nolie got to decide what she and Dad ordered in for dinner that night. She chose Chinese because they hadn't had it in a while. And because she liked her chicken and broccoli slathered in sauce. When Linden was home, they split it, and had to order it plain because Linden didn't like the sauce. And even though Nolie would get a whole tub of sauce on the side, it never tasted as yummy as it did when the restaurant sent it already mixed in.

But for some reason, that night, when Dad called Mr. Tang's to order, he said, "One sesame beef and one steamed chicken and broccoli with extra sauce on the side."

"Da-ad!" Nolie shouted. "Sauce on top. Sautéed, not steamed!"

"One second," he said, taking the phone from his ear and placing it against his chest to muffle their voices because he could never find the mute button. "Maybe your sister will have some leftovers for tomorrow."

"Yeah, but it's *my* order tonight, so I should get it *my* way." Nolie knew she was acting like a bratty toddler at Joey's, but her chest felt tight, and her stomach clenched with the injustice. Even when Linden wasn't there, she was getting it *her* way? "But do whatever! I'll starve to death!"

Dad looked at the phone, and then at Nolie, and then back to the phone again. "Sorry," he said to the restaurant. "We're having a moment. Call you right back."

He put down the phone. Facedown on the table, so he could focus just on her. "What's up, Nolie? What's the big deal?"

She shied away from his stare, from how deeply he was looking at her.

"I just want it my way. Okay?"

Dad inhaled loudly through his nose. "I see that this is really important to you, even though you've always been fine ordering sauce on the side before. But is this really about the sauce?"

It was a rhetorical question. Dad shook his head, redialed the restaurant, and finished their order. The way Nolie wanted it.

Nolie'd won. She'd made her point about getting her way. But it didn't feel like a victory. Maybe it was about more than the food. Maybe it was about how nothing seemed to be going her way. Cousins Week got cut short, Jessa wanted her to be Magnolia, and her family's whole life revolved around what Linden wanted. And Nolie was expected to go along with it all.

Her chicken and broccoli dish arrived cold, for the first time ever. And it had too much spice to make it enjoyable to eat. She ended up scraping off a lot of the sauce anyway, and heating it up in the microwave.

After a less than satisfactory meal, Nolie ripped

open the plastic wrapper of her fortune cookie, took in a whiff of the sugary crunchiness, and cracked it in half.

Empty.

Not even a blank slip of paper.

Nothing.

Which had happened to Dad once before at the restaurant. He'd asked Mr. Tang what it meant when you got an empty fortune cookie.

"Ah," Mr. Tang said, chin lifted as he made his proclamation: "Either the cup fills over, or the cup is empty."

Mom and Dad nodded like Mr. Tang said something super wise, but Nolie didn't get it.

"My interpretation," Dad explained as they walked home after dinner, "is that you can look at it one of two ways. The optimistic way is that your cup fills over—life is so full, you don't need anything else. Or, the pessimistic way is that your cup is empty; you have nothing."

"My cup is full," Linden declared, a satisfied look on her face. "I don't need anything more."

Mom agreed. She was too scientific minded to

believe in fortunes anyway. And Dad made a corny joke about how his life was full of his wonderful wife and daughters.

Nolie'd wanted to agree that her cup was full, too, but she wasn't so sure. Sometimes her cup felt kind of empty.

And now it'd happened to her. She'd gotten the empty fortune cookie.

Dad crunched down on his cookie and read out his fortune. *"Believe in your abilities, confidence leads the way.* I guess the fortune cookie gods know that my Nolie doesn't need platitudes to help her find her way."

Nolie tried to smile, but she didn't even feel like eating her cookie anymore. She pushed the pieces over to Dad.

"You sure?" he asked, before he popped another bite into his mouth.

Nolie nodded. She worried that Dad had got it all wrong. That the fortune cookie gods were trying to tell her that she was the one whose cup was empty. And if she ate that empty shell of a cookie, she'd never figure out how to fill her cup.

* * *

That night Linden spent what felt like hours prepping her desk and school stuff for her first day of seventh grade. She lined up her file folders in a plastic holder on her desk, organized by color and subject, and made sure her binder was in order with labeled dividers and her pencil pouch was full of freshly sharpened pencils.

"What's that?" Linden asked, noticing the Magnolia pouch on top of Nolie's backpack. Nolie hadn't even bothered sharpening the pencils she'd put inside it—the ones she had from last year were sharp enough, for now.

"Jessa." Nolie couldn't hide the negativity in her voice.

"So pretentious," Linden said, rubbing lotion into her callused feet.

"What do you mean?"

"I mean, that girl is way too mature for her own good. She's wanted to be a teenager since she was seven years old. Didn't she start wearing a bra last year before she even really needed it? Seriously, what's the rush?"

"Well, she needs a bra now," Nolie said. Nolie herself wasn't in any rush, and she knew Linden wasn't, either.

For Linden, becoming a teenager meant the end of dancing the children's roles in ballet. It meant pushing herself to train harder and harder to make it into summer intensives and a preprofessional program and an apprenticeship with a company.

"Why did she put *Magnolia*?" Linden asked. "It's not like anyone calls you that."

Nolie groaned. "It's her big idea to call me Magnolia this year. Do you think it sounds more mature?"

"No," Linden scoffed. "It makes you sound like a doll in a toy shop. Or some sort of hippie flower child. No way."

That wasn't exactly a vote of confidence in Nolie being who she already was. But it was definitely *not* a vote for her to try out being Magnolia.

Later, after Linden was asleep, Nolie took her dull pencils from the Magnolia pouch and fished last year's pencil pouch out of her drawer. It was a boring solid color blue, frayed in the corners, and the zipper got stuck. So it would've been nice to have a new pouch for sixth grade. But she didn't *need* it. Not when it had the name of someone she wasn't.

Instead, she stuffed the Magnolia pouch where it belonged: in the closet, in her bag of discarded things.

4

COOLER COOLER COOLER

Sixth grade shouldn't have made Nolie nervous. She'd been in the same, too small, all-girls school with mostly the same girls since kindergarten.

Fifth grade was the year that middle school had officially started. The main differences were they went from wearing plaid uniform jumpers to plaid kilts, they moved up to the third and fourth floors of the red-brick school building, and switched classes for every subject. And a few new girls had started. Last year, Nolie wasn't nervous because she'd had Jessa.

Now, in the third floor locker hallway before first bell, everyone else seemed so happy to be back for the first day of school. The chatter and laughter of throngs of girls echoed off the cinderblock walls and linoleum floor. The noise had the effect of making Nolie feel like she was underwater, a fish lost and looking for its shoal.

Some girls decorated the insides of their lockers with mirrors and stickers and photographs, like it was their own space for self-expression. Nolie suddenly realized she hadn't brought anything special for hers. She hadn't known that would be a thing this year. She took extra long taping her printed-out class schedule to the inside door of her puke green locker, as if that added a super-personal touch, and took out the books she needed for her morning classes.

Nolie finally spotted Jessa and Calliope huddled together at Jessa's locker down the hall. Their blue and burgundy plaid kilts were definitely a few fingers too high for uniform regulation, and the collars of their polo shirts unbuttoned and popped up, like all the popular girls. She caught sight of the inside of Jessa's locker door, which was covered in photographs. She wasn't close enough to make out any of the faces in them, but she didn't see any dark-haired girls, like her. From a distance, everyone in Jessa's photographs looked blond.

Nolie tried to push her way through the sea of girls between them before homeroom bell rang. Just as she was within arm's reach of Jessa, the loud buzz jolted everyone into action and girls scrambled in all directions to get to homeroom. No one wanted to be late on the first day, and possibly get stuck in a bad seat.

"Sit with you at lunch?" Nolie called out to Jessa as a crowd of girls swarmed by, pushing them apart.

"Yeah," Jessa called back, before she turned left toward Mr. Fink's room. But not with a longing or sad look, or a hand reaching wistfully toward Nolie, like she would've done last year if they'd been separated that way.

Homeroom and the rest of the morning was uneventful. The usual discussions about their summers and expectations for the year. Nolie tuned out, looking around at the other girls, trying to figure out who she could possibly be friends with. None of them were girls she'd been friendly with before. Maybe because she'd always had Jessa.

Somehow, while Jessa was Nolie's one and only

best friend, Jessa had managed to make other friends besides Nolie. It was like they were on a seesaw, and Jessa's end of the seesaw was always on the ground, while Nolie's end was high up in the air, wavering dangerously, because she had no one to help bring her side down.

Some of the girls were definitely *not* on her list of possible friends. Girls who had silly nicknames that Jessa had made up for them last year. Maddie Chu— Mindful Maddie. She'd gotten all yoga and meditation obsessed and even started her own video channel. Bridget Lowey, also known as Booboo Bridget. Any time she got the slightest scrape or cut at school, she cried and went to the nurse. Jessa had even given Linden a nickname: Lucky Linden.

And Shady Serena. She was new last year, like Calliope, but unlike Calliope, Serena made zero effort to get to know the girls, or to fit in. Her blond hair frizzed wildly, unless she clipped it down with babyish plastic barrettes or headbands, and sometimes she wore blue-framed glasses that made her pale skin look even more ghostly. Serena kept to herself, which was why Jessa called her shady, but she spoke up in class, and always had the right answer when teachers called on her.

At lunch the dining hall smelled of French fries and burgers like it always did on the first day of school. The burgers were thin and floppy, nothing like the thick, juicy ones they grilled at Grandma's beach cottage. Nolie spotted Jessa and Calliope at a round table with some other girls in the corner. The table that Jessa had been too slow to claim as hers last year, but she'd clearly rushed to nab this year. Vivian Johnson, who had straightened her signature puffs, and also seemed to have gotten blond highlights, and Calliope sat on either side of Jessa. Nolie sat across from her. Two points on a circle, opposite ends of the diameter.

"Hey, Noles." The nickname only Jessa and Linden used for her. It made her feel warm, like the Magnolia thing had been forgotten. Like Jessa was still *hers* even if she was spending more time with her other friends.

Calliope butted in with, "Don't you mean *Magnolia*? Magnificent Magnolia?" She flashed a smile that was directed toward Nolie, but clearly more for Jessa's benefit.

Wait. Was *Nolie* getting nicknamed now? Would they be calling her Magnificent Magnolia behind her back? But *magnificent* was a positive thing, right? Unless—more likely—Calliope meant it in a sarcastic way. To turn Nolie into a joke.

Jessa slapped her hand to her forehead. "Of course. *Magnolia*," she said. And she continued whatever story she'd been in the middle of telling. Without bothering to fill Nolie in on what she'd missed. Something about Ms. Tapper farting in science class and trying to cover it up with an exploding volcano experiment.

Even from across the table, as Jessa made exaggerated hand gestures to tell her story, a scent wafted up Nolie's nose. The same heavy sweet perfume that she'd sprayed for Nolie last year, in her mom's bathroom. She told Nolie that Andie wore it when she went out on dates. They'd laughed about how any guy could possibly get close to her when she smelled like *that*. Like sugar.

Nolie played with the seashell on her necklace, not really thinking about it, to distract herself, until Jessa finished the story.

Jessa cocked her head. "You're still wearing that

necklace?" she asked, as if Nolie had mortally offended her.

"Yeah." Nolie dropped the seashell, fast.

"I told you, that kind of hurt my feelings. Right?"

Calliope looked between them, trying to follow the conversation. Nolie's cheeks burned. She hadn't meant to offend Jessa by wearing it. But it was easy enough not to wear it, if it was that big of a deal to her best friend.

"Fine," Nolie said, tucking it into her shirt. Even though it felt all wrong.

"Thanks," Jessa said dramatically. "You know how *this* defines me." She gripped her crystal like it was her very heart beating in her fingers.

Nolie gave an inward eyeroll, while Calliope nodded in sympathy for Jessa's feelings.

After lunch, Jessa pulled Nolie aside on the way to their next classes. "Here, this is for you." She pressed a tightly folded piece of notepaper into Nolie's hand.

A sheet of Jessa's special lavender-colored notepaper with her name printed in purple across the top, two hearts on either side. It was the perfect size notepaper— large enough to write all you wanted to say, but small enough that it could be folded into a trim little square and put in your pocket.

"For now, or later?" Nolie asked. Sometimes, last spring, Jessa would write funny notes to Nolie. Nothing too mean, just silly observations she'd made throughout the day, such as girls who were being goody-goodies, or teachers that bored her. She'd always tell Nolie if it was a note for now—okay to open and read right away—or for later. Something to hide in her backpack and read only in private.

"Either way." Jessa shrugged.

Nolie raised her eyebrows. Jessa never left things up to chance.

Curiosity got the best of Nolie. She unfolded the note and started to read as they reached the door to her next class.

Jessa'd written the words in dark blue ink, in her bubbly round handwriting: *The Magnolia Self-Improvement Project*.

"Good idea, right?" Jessa watched Nolie read.

There were three items on the list:

> *1) Stop wearing your hair pulled tight in a ponytail.*

2) Eat less sweets.

3) Pay more attention to your clothes—kilt
   too long!!!

Well, Nolie hated the feel of her hair in her face, she
had no desire to stop eating sweets—or whatever else
she wanted, for that matter—and clothes were boring.
In fact, the idea of flashing her thighs for the world to
see the way that Jessa did held absolutely zero appeal.

Nolie made a half grin, half grimace. No point in
arguing with Jessa. She always thought she was right,
even when she wasn't. But eventually, she'd see things
Nolie's way.

At least, she used to.

"It's a start," Jessa said to her silence. "Along with
the whole *Magnolia* thing. Something for us to work
on together. You know, like a makeover."

"A makeover? You mean a spa day?" Nolie
scrunched her nose. She could *feel* the seeds poking
through the cold slices of cucumber Jessa'd placed on
her closed eyes; the lumpiness of the blueberry yogurt
she'd rubbed all over her face, last time they did a
"spa day." Nope. Not for Nolie.

Jessa couldn't pay her to do that again. Good thing

Jessa had Calliope—maybe she was into food-based spa treatments.

"Oh, relax, Magnolia. That's the whole point—to make you more fun."

"Gee, thanks," Nolie said. She stuffed the list into her backpack.

"That part—about making you more fun—was Calliope's idea," Jessa blurted out. And then she leaned in, to whisper: "She told me that she thinks you could be cooler."

Knowing that Calliope was involved, that they'd discussed Nolie behind her back, and that it was *her* idea, made it worse.

What did "cooler" even mean? The more Nolie said it, over and over in her head—*cooler cooler cooler*—it didn't even sound like a real word. It made her think of pigeons cooing and baby's babbling.

Did she even want to be cooler? And would calling herself Magnolia and following Jessa's list work? Or was she fine just being herself—being Nolie?

"How was your day?" Linden asked on their way home.

Nolie didn't want anyone to know the truth, especially not Linden, who might let it slip by accident. There was the time last year when Nolie got hit with a stomach bug and threw up on the public bus. Linden helped her clean up, and even put her arm around Nolie in support the whole way home despite the stink. But then, Linden had told the story in one of her classes—she claimed she didn't think anyone would laugh at Nolie about it. And now some of the girls in Linden's grade held their noses and pretended to gag whenever Nolie walked by.

But Nolie couldn't think of anything else to tell Linden about her first day. It was the only thing that came out of her mouth: Jessa and the necklace and the list and *cooler*.

"Really, Noles?" Linden shook her head. "Doesn't sound like something a best friend should do."

"Whatever," Nolie said. "It's just Jessa. You take the good with the bad."

There'd always been a mix of good and bad about Jessa. Last fall, for example, Jessa'd convinced Nolie to sneak into a PG-13 movie after Andie had dropped them off at the theater to watch a PG princess movie.

The movie was so much better than what they were supposed to see, and the thrill of sneaking in made Nolie's head rush like she was on an upside-down roller coaster. But then there was the bad that came after: Nolie couldn't help but confess the truth to her mom, who suggested that Nolie tell Jessa that she'd told, and that Jessa should tell *her* mom, too. But Jessa had refused, and gotten mad at Nolie instead. She didn't speak to her for what felt like weeks after that. Maybe that's when she'd started to become friends with Calliope.

"I don't know," Linden said. "You could try to branch out a bit? Make some other friends?"

Unlike Nolie, Linden didn't have one best friend. She had lots of girls who she called close friends. In her grade at school, she'd use that title for at least five girls, and at ballet, she had Charlotte Fitzroy, who was sometimes a close friend, other times a rival. They both wanted to be Marie that year. Nolie was holding her breath they both got it, or there would be all-out misery. If one of Linden's close friends acted toward her the way that Jessa was acting toward Nolie, Linden would have someone else to turn to.

Not to mention that none of Linden's friends would ever tell her not to wear a certain necklace or make her the subject of a self-improvement project. Linden was already perfect. Nolie and Linden were only fourteen months apart, but it was like the best of everything their parents had was put into Linden. Once when they were in a big fight over something Nolie didn't even remember, Linden said since Mom got pregnant so quickly after she was born, her body didn't have time to recover and make anything good for Nolie. Whatever that meant. But it had stuck with her.

"Remember when you were friends with Maddie Chu in first grade?" Linden went on. "She was nice."

"Mindful Maddie?" Nolie snorted.

"Is that what they call her?"

"Yeah, because she's yoga and meditation obsessed."

"What's so bad about that? At least she's chill." Linden shrugged. "You'll figure it out."

Easy enough for Linden to say. Linden always knew exactly what she wanted, and how to get it. Like her determination with ballet. She went to class every day and practiced and practiced so she'd be good enough to try for the starring role, which she'd probably get. She even threw herself with passion into her bat mitzvah prep, which most kids, including their cousin Anna, found a chore.

Maybe if Nolie had some passion she worked for, she'd know what to do, too. A direction to go in. A path to follow.

She could follow Jessa, and be Magnolia, and tick off the items on the self-improvement list. But at home, she pulled out Jessa's list and couldn't even bring herself to reread it. Instead, she shredded it to bits of lavender confetti over the kitchen counter and dumped the pieces into the trash. And then she ate a few Chips Ahoy for a snack and watched TV since she didn't have any homework yet.

Before she showered that night, she took off her seashell necklace, like she always did for bed. She loved how it reminded her of her happy place at Grandma's beach cottage.

Why should she listen to Jessa? Why shouldn't she have a special necklace to wear from her grandma, too?

She sighed. Because she knew if she continued to

wear it, and Jessa said more mean things about it to her, the mean comments would sink into her heart and take away some of the joy of the necklace for her. It would turn the necklace into a fight with Jessa that she didn't want to have. So she put it on the windowsill, next to Linden's necklace. To keep it safe from anyone ruining it for her.

Later that night, Nolie finally got a chance to be alone with Mom. She came in to say good night while Linden was in the living room finishing an English essay.

"Mom?" Nolie said in her softest, most heartfelt voice. She knew Mom was tired, but she was always open to having deep discussions about life issues.

"Hmm?" Mom stood in the doorway, arms crossed, eyelids half shut, breathing in deeply through her nose and out through her mouth, like she was falling asleep on her feet. Or trying to keep calm.

Mom worked super hard. She was a geriatric nurse, which meant she took care of old people who needed a private nurse at home. Mr. Weiler was Mom's current patient, for the last five years. Nolie sometimes went there after school when she had nothing else to do.

She loved Mr. Weiler's apartment. There was a whole room called the library. It had bookshelves stuffed to the brim and smelled of book bindings and paper. A worn sofa sagged on the end where Mr. Weiler used to sit, when he still could. In recent years his health had declined, so he spent more time half conscious in a hospital bed than in his library. Mom had to lift him to clean him and change him like a baby; her back and arms ached at the end of every day.

That night, as Mom stood in Nolie's doorway to say good night, and Nolie was figuring out how to tell her about what'd happened with Jessa, Mom's phone buzzed. Not once, but three times, rapidly. Like it was urgent. Mom pulled out her phone and looked at the message. Her forehead pinched in irritation.

"Ugh. Got to deal with some insurance paperwork. So sorry, sweetheart. Give me a few minutes and I'll be right back."

But Nolie fell asleep before Mom returned.

There was no time to talk to Mom in the morning, during the mad rush to get out the door to work and school.

Besides, it felt different in the morning. Like

maybe there wasn't really anything to tell Mom about.

Sure, Jessa was acting kind of rude, but maybe it'd get better. Maybe she'd drop the idea of making Nolie cooler, and remember how they'd always been.

But it didn't get better. The rest of that week, Jessa made a point of calling her Magnolia and correcting her behavior. "A few inches, pretty please?"—she said grabbing at Nolie's kilt to roll the waistband over. "No snickerdoodles for you today!"—even though they were Nolie's favorite. And, "Pretty please, let me braid your hair or something?"

It wasn't much fun for Nolie, being friends with someone who only seemed to want to make her transform into another kind of girl. A girl who wasn't Nolie.

5

A JEWISH MARIE?

On Sunday morning, Nolie huddled deep under her covers and buried her ears in her pillow to muffle the noise of Linden getting ready for her audition for *The Nutcracker*.

Nolie tried to stay in her dreams. She fell in and out of sleep as Linden yelled at Mom not to yank while running the brush through her long, thick hair, taming and twisting it into a tight bun. She ignored the smell of Linden's protein-filled breakfast of scrambled eggs and sausage, wafting from the kitchen to her room. It was only seven a.m.! Way too early for this much noise and energy on a weekend morning.

Finally Nolie dragged herself out of bed to eat the leftovers of breakfast. She was just in time to see Mom and Linden leave. Linden with her ballet duffel slung over her shoulder, Mom with a book shoved in her bag.

Nolie knew how it would go. Mom would sit on one of those plastic molded chairs, clutching the closed book on her lap. She'd want to read but wouldn't be able to concentrate. Instead, she'd chat nervously with the other parents, while the ballerinas danced their hearts out.

Thankfully, for everyone, they didn't have to wait through days of nail-biting nerves on Linden's behalf. The casting for Marie would be announced at the end of the day.

"Want to come to Joey's with me today?" Dad asked, raising his eyebrows at Nolie over his fourth cup of coffee.

Dad went to the store even on Sundays. Especially on Sundays, he said, because that was one of their busiest days. Nolie didn't know why he had to work on the weekends, when his family'd owned the business for years. But he was hands on that way.

She considered. It's not as if she had anything else to do. And being home alone on Sunday—a day that she imagined other families spent together in pajamas, watching TV while their parents read the papers, savoring a leisurely brunch—wasn't her idea of fun.

"C'mon," Dad said, sensing her hesitation. "You can do the balloons."

The store would be super busy. There'd be a lot of balloons to hand out.

So Nolie said yes.

Dad hummed cheerfully as they walked, swinging a trademark Joey's Shoes shopping bag with their lunches in it. Turkey and lettuce and tomato with mayo on rye for him. Swiss and lettuce and tomato on whole wheat for Nolie.

On Sunday mornings Dad always got a carton of pastries delivered before opening as a treat for the salespeople. That morning there were two mini chocolate croissants left for Nolie. A perfect way to start the day.

The first couple hours sped by. Lots of little kids. Some tiny ones, getting their first pair of walkers. And too many toddlers, who ran around and couldn't keep their grimy fingers off the display shoes.

When they didn't need Nolie on the sales floor, she blew up balloons in the back office. Her favorite part was the zap of helium going in. Then tying off the balloon as cleanly as she could and choosing a color string to go with each one. She even made a loop at the ends of the strings so the little kids could wear them around their wrists or secure them to their strollers or scooters. Though of course there was always the sobbing kid whose parents had to bring them back for a replacement because their balloon had flown away.

Right before lunch a frazzled-looking but dressed up mom came in, causing a commotion as she wielded two babies in a double stroller and a toddler perched on a ride-on board. And an older girl with blond hair, about Nolie's age.

The last person Nolie'd want to see in *her* store.

Calliope.

Jessa's Calliope. Wearing a flouncy dress that was better suited for a special occasion than for a lazy Sunday. Oh, right. Sunday meant church. And Sunday school. With Jessa.

Calliope's eyes widened with surprise when she

saw Nolie standing by the checkout counter.

Not that she should be surprised. Or maybe she should—Calliope had only started at their school last year after moving from Florida. But still. *Everyone* knew that Nolie's dad owned Joey's.

This was Nolie's turf. She stood up straighter, threw back her shoulders, and marched up to Calliope's family.

"Welcome to Joey's." Nolie flashed her biggest salesperson smile at the mom, who wore high heels, dangly earrings, and gobs of makeup while taking care of all those little kids. No wonder she was so frazzled.

Nolie figured she could help pick out some cute sneakers for the toddler. Or tell Calliope's mom to get a head start on buying winter boots. Joey's did a buy-two-get-one-half-off sale for winter boots in September. Maybe she was the type to prepare early. In any case, Nolie was ready to impress with her shoe know-how.

The mom barely registered Nolie's positive energy, though, as one of the babies in the stroller arched its back and threw up its arms, wailing like a fire alarm.

"We need shoes," the mom gasped as she wrangled

up the baby, who was twisted in the stroller straps. "You have her size?" She tilted her head toward Calliope.

Calliope? She wanted Nolie to help Calliope buy shoes?

"Um, sure," Nolie said, trying to meet Calliope's eyes. But Calliope was glued to her phone, texting furiously. Probably telling Jessa how embarrassing it was that "Magnificent Magnolia," the most uncool person they knew, was supposed to help her with shoes.

One glance at Calliope's white sneakers with a sparkly gold logo, which made her flouncy church dress look fashionably edgy, and Nolie knew right away. Joey's didn't carry things like that.

She felt Dad watching her from behind the glass window of the office. A surge of pride rose up in Nolie for all those shoes lined up on display on the walls.

"What kind of shoes do you need?" Nolie asked.

Calliope finally looked up from her phone and at Nolie. Looked her up and down, more like it. "I'm not sure this is the store for me. Seems like you specialize in *baby* shoes."

"Not true." Nolie swept her arms grandly around the store, as if she was the hostess on a game show. One of Dad's lines rolled off her tongue: "We've got great choices for all ages."

"Mom," Calliope whined. "Can we go somewhere else? Please?" She sounded desperate.

The mom shook her head, and rocked impatiently in her pointy high heels. The diamond drops on her hoop earrings shimmered. "We just got here. You haven't even tried anything on yet."

"There's nothing I want here," Calliope insisted. "Let's go." And before the mom could get the baby settled back into the stroller, Calliope had turned on her trendy sneaker heels and marched out.

"Sorry," the mom said to Nolie, pinching the bridge of her nose. "We'll try another time!"

Calliope didn't bother to hold the door for her mom, who struggled to maneuver the stroller. So Nolie held it open for her. The mom's appreciative smile was a small consolation.

Nolie turned back into Joey's, feeling empty inside. Her stomach growled. She glanced down at her phone. No messages, but it was time for lunch. She plopped down at Dad's office desk to eat their sandwiches together.

"You know that girl?" Dad asked. "The one with all the little siblings?"

"Kind of," Nolie said. "Why?"

"Don't know. She looked about your age."

Nolie shrugged and chewed her sandwich.

"We didn't have anything they wanted?" Dad asked.

Nolie didn't want to make him feel bad. "I think the baby had a dirty diaper or something."

"Did you tell the mom we have a changing table in our bathroom?"

"Yeah, but they were in a hurry. Besides, she's in my grade at school. She's . . . not the nicest."

"Got it," Dad said. He went back to eating and checked his phone.

Nolie kind of wished he would ask another question, like, "Why isn't she the nicest?"

She wished she could tell him that not only wasn't Calliope the nicest, but also that she thought Nolie needed to be *cooler*. And she was stealing Jessa.

But Dad didn't seem interested in knowing those

things. Or he didn't ask the right follow-up questions. Mom and Linden would, if they were there. But they weren't.

Linden's *Nutcracker* audition was way more important than Nolie's shoe-selling fail with Calliope.

It was like on the first day of school, when she'd wanted to tell Mom about Jessa and the Magnolia self-improvement project. It had felt important to Nolie when it happened, but then the next morning, it seemed to matter less.

Or at least, it seemed like something that Mom wouldn't really understand. The kind of thing not worth telling about.

Something that she could manage, on her own.

Near closing time that afternoon, Linden's voice, unmistakably joyful, burst out of Dad's speakerphone: "Meet us at Grandma's!"

"To celebrate?" Dad asked. Nolie took in a deep, hopeful breath, her lungs about to burst. She felt as anxious on Linden's behalf as everyone else did.

"Eeek! Yes! I got it! I got it!" Muffled voices,

cheers, laughter, words of congratulations sounded in the background as Linden handed the phone to Mom.

"She did it!" Mom said. "Our girl! Marie, here we come!"

Nolie'd never heard Mom so elated, ever. Not even the time she'd lost her engagement ring and Nolie had found it for her, in her pants pocket.

Even Nolie felt a flutter of excitement, like it was happening to her. Linden was going to be Marie! The star of the New York City Ballet's production of *The Nutcracker*. Onstage for the entire two-hour performance, in front of thousands of people at Lincoln Center. It was the kind of thing that changed your life, made you famous.

Her sister. Linden Beck.

They met at Grandma's for a celebratory dinner. Grandma's apartment felt sacred to Nolie. It was the same apartment that Dad and Aunt Eve had grown up in.

City Grandma was always more sophisticated than Beach Grandma. City Grandma got her hair done at the salon, smoothed off her forehead in a pouf, and wore dark eyeliner, red lipstick, and gold bracelets that jangled on her wrist. She pulled Nolie into a hug, but Nolie worried about messing up Grandma's hair or getting a red lipstick print on her cheek. Still, in the city or at the beach, she was the same Grandma. Her soapy, floral scent and the sound of opera playing softly through the speakers of her old stereo made Nolie's chest expand, her shoulders relax.

Grandma's apartment was on a low floor overlooking Central Park, so you could see green through the windows, but they were smaller and narrow, not like the wide openness of the beach cottage. The dark wood floor was covered in antique rugs, the living room packed with bookshelves and small paintings and tables full of treasures: lacquered and enameled boxes, decorative porcelain, a brass magnifying glass and letter opener.

And Nolie's favorite, a compass. Nolie's great-great-grandfather had brought it with him when he emigrated from Russia to New York. Nolie loved to hold that compass—the glass all scratchy and foggy, the intricate engraving on the back. In Nolie's hands it felt smooth and cool, like a large stone. She watched how the arrow quivered until it settled on magnetic north.

Mom and Grandma ordered dinner over the phone from Linden's favorite Japanese restaurant. Dad broke out a bottle of champagne and gave them each a few sips.

Linden glowed with happiness. As they gathered in the living room, waiting for the food to arrive, she told and retold the details of the audition. How the rehearsal directors kept them in suspense until the end. How it came down to her and her friend Charlotte Fitzroy and a few others. And Linden and Charlotte both got cast as Marie—one for the Red cast, and one for the Green cast, so they'd rotate performances. It all worked out perfectly, and the whole thing was a dream come true.

"So, are you the first Jewish Marie?" Grandma asked.

"There've been Jewish Maries before," Linden said. "I think. We're a pretty diverse cast, Grandma. We're from all over the city, all kinds of backgrounds. My prince, Milo, is half Black, half Korean." At the mention of her prince, Linden's cheeks pinked up.

"Crush, maybe?" Nolic asked.

Linden brushed her off. "No flirting among cast members. That's an official rule."

"Sure," Nolie teased as Linden's face grew redder.

"But yeah, he is super cute." She was full-on blushing now.

"I can vouch for that," Mom said.

"Diverse cast or not," Grandma said, "I need to make sure you two stay Jewish enough. What with your Christmas show and not even having enough time to go to Hebrew school."

Grandma always said going to see *The Nutcracker* was a Christmas tradition and not part of her religion. She only went because her granddaughter was performing in it. And Linden was the one who didn't have time to attend Hebrew school because the classes were held on Wednesdays, when she had ballet. Nolie would've had time, but because Linden didn't go, it was easier for her not to go, either. So Linden met with a tutor on Thursday evenings, instead, that the synagogue had arranged for her. Nolie would start with the tutor soon, too. After Linden's bat mitzvah.

"C'mon, Grandma," Linden said. "I'm not going to change my name like Alicia Markova."

The mention of that name gave Nolie a shiver of worry. Alicia Markova was Linden's personal hero.

The first famous openly Jewish, British ballerina. The first Jewish ballerina to dance the Sugar Plum Fairy in a production of *The Nutcracker* in the United States. Linden was outraged when Grandma had given her an article a couple years ago about how Alicia had been convinced to change her name to succeed in her career: she was born Lillian Alicia Marks but was told that to make it as a ballerina in the 1920s, you had to sound Russian. Hence, Alicia Markova.

Linden was going to make the most amazing sermon linking her Torah portion to Alicia's name change and groundbreaking career. Linden swore she'd never change herself or her identity to succeed. Ever.

And Nolie knew that Linden's bat mitzvah sermon would be perfect, just like everything else Linden did. Everyone was going to say how impressive she was, how insightful, what a good writer.

Nolie's bat mitzvah would only be a year later. And she had no personal hero or passion to focus on for her sermon.

Everyone would praise Nolie, too, but they wouldn't mean it. They'd say it because they had to. Because that's what you did when someone worked hard to prepare for an event like a bat mitzvah—you said "Mazel tov" and how well they did.

As Linden went on and on about the auditions, the history of Jewish ballerinas, and all the other fascinating parts of her life, Mom and Dad sat there beaming. They could listen to her all day. They practically lived it with her. And even though Nolie was proud to be the sister of the star, eventually her patience for it ran out. How many times could you listen to your sister say the same things over and over? Glow with happiness at how perfect everything was for her.

No one even bothered to ask Dad and Nolie how *their* day had been. Whether there was any news to report from Joey's. Not that there would've been much to tell, anyway. The most interesting thing had been her run-in with Calliope, and what could she say about that? It would just take away from the excitement around Linden.

But that night, Nolie made sure to text Jessa the big news about Linden. Even if Jessa thought Nolie needed improving, she was still in awe of Linden, like all the girls in middle school. They didn't have to say it, but Nolie knew they wondered how she and Linden could be sisters.

OMG!!! Lucky Linden! Jessa texted back immediately. *When can we go? I'm dying to go behind the scenes this year.*

Nolie'd promised Jessa last year that she could come with them to one of the performances. Even though being the family of a performer in *The Nutcracker* wasn't as exciting as it sounded.

It meant a lot of sitting around backstage, in a big room with the other families and kid dancers. You watched the show from a monitor screen in the backstage room because you still had to pay for real tickets to sit in the audience.

All that happened in that big backstage room was the kid dancers running around, getting ready. Mom, who wore no makeup herself—or sometimes even Dad, if Mom wasn't available—had to put on Linden's makeup and do her hair. Though Linden started doing it herself last year.

Nolie would sit in the corner the times she had to go, pretending to read or draw or do homework.

Trying to ignore all those ballet kids warming up, squealing with excitement, acting like they were at a big, important party. One that Nolie couldn't possibly be part of, being a mere sister of a performer.

Even though Nolie'd promised to bring Jessa, she kept making excuses for why she couldn't. Until Jessa came and saw how boring it was in real life, Nolie could still pretend it was actually exciting. That being Linden's sister made her special.

Because these days, being Lucky Linden's sister was starting to seem like the only thing magnificent about her.

6

THE OTHER SIDE OF SHADY

On Monday morning a group of girls, each holding a single red rose, gathered at Linden's locker. They practically worshipped at Linden's feet, asking her all the questions about the audition, and exclaiming "How cool!," "How amazing!," "How awesome—Marie!"

Even Jessa was there to watch. "Edie bought a dozen roses at the bodega on the way to school. And they're each giving her one."

How sweet. Linden had enough friends for each one to give her a rose from that dozen. If Nolie ever had something to celebrate, it'd be Jessa alone giving her a flower. One single, measly rose. If Jessa even cared to celebrate Nolie ever again. Now she was more likely to give a criticism than a compliment.

"Linden is too perfect," Jessa said wistfully, watching the older girls glom around her.

Linden did look pretty near perfect. She wore her kilt a few inches too high, to show off her legs. Like Jessa, but not short enough to get her into trouble. After checking to make sure no one was watching, Nolie rolled her waistband over once, to hike up her kilt the tiniest bit extra. To see if maybe it would make a difference, make her cooler.

At the same time, if anyone should know that Linden was far from perfect, it was Jessa. Jessa'd slept over plenty of times. She'd crouch in her corner of the couch while they were trying to watch a movie as Linden yelled at Nolie for some reason or another—using her toothbrush by mistake, borrowing a T-shirt without asking, messing up her index cards by accident. Jessa'd seen Linden rage at Mom when she didn't get her ballet hairstyle fixed exactly right.

Now, Jessa refocused her attention on Nolie.

"Magnolia, the list!" she whispered. "Hair, down!"

Nolie rolled her kilt up one more time, and slid the band off her ponytail, pulling out the few extra strands tangled in the elastic and dropping them to the floor. She gave her head a little shake and ran her fingers through her hair.

Jessa lifted up Nolie's hair, like she was inspecting her for lice. "Um, I don't know. You took a shower this morning, right?"

Nolie shook her head.

"Last night?"

"Maybe." Truth was, Nolie might not have showered since Friday. She didn't need to shower if she hadn't done exercise or anything to get sweaty.

"I don't know. I mean, your hair kind of smells. It looks greasy. Maybe it's better if you put it back up."

"Or should I do twenty jumping jacks and drop for push-ups? I mean, seriously, Jessa."

"I am serious." Jessa looked away from Nolie. "Sometimes you kind of embarrass me."

Maybe Jessa didn't actually just say that. But from the redness in Jessa's cheeks, creeping down her neck, Nolie knew that she did. And that she meant it.

Was Nolie that bad?

How could this person, who she'd always turned

to, could always count on as her best friend, be embarrassed by her? And since when?

A nervous flutter welled up inside Nolie. Linden was right. A real friend, a best friend, wouldn't treat you this way. Unless she was sincerely trying to help. But deep inside, Nolie didn't think she needed that kind of help.

And as her insides all tore up, she burst into nervous laughter. Which led to uncontrollable giggles, which sounded like a choking hyena, which turned to hiccupping. She couldn't stop.

"Magnolia? You okay? Water! Drink!" Jessa pulled Nolie's water bottle from the outside pocket of her backpack and handed it to her.

The water got Nolie's breath back to normal. "Thanks."

"Calliope said you haven't used the pencil pouch I got you. Why not?"

Nolie computed that—Calliope reporting on her. "Um, I don't know. I guess I forgot."

"Really? I thought hard about those gifts. I paid for them with my allowance money."

"Sorry, but—" The homeroom bell rang.

Nolie didn't even say her usual "See ya at lunch" to Jessa. If she tried to speak again, she'd end up in another fit of hiccups.

All through math class, the hiccups came and went. Elinor Fowler and Shady Serena, the girls who sat on either side of her, gave Nolie questioning looks. She even felt Calliope watch her from across the room. She took out her faded blue pencil pouch and tucked it protectively under her notebook, away from Calliope's judging stare.

"Do you need to excuse yourself and get some water?" Mr. Dundas asked once Nolie hiccupped so loud it drew notice from the entire class. It was a relief to leave in the middle of class to refill her water bottle at the fountain in the empty hallway. Empty, except for the principal, who noticed that Nolie's skirt was rolled up and asked her to lower it.

At lunch the hiccups grew stronger. Each hiccup jolted the plate of grilled cheese and soggy peas on the brown vinyl lunch tray.

It was a no-good, horrible, very bad day. Nolie desperately needed to sit, to take a few big gulps of water.

But even though there was an empty seat waiting for her, Jessa's table didn't beckon to her like a safe haven. As she got near, she saw the sneers on Jessa and Calliope's faces, and she couldn't bring herself to be a part of it.

For all she knew, the faces they were making, the whispers, were about her. Maybe they were writing another list of how to improve Magnolia. Of all the things she was supposed to do that she wasn't—like shower every day and use her personalized pencil pouch.

There had to be other girls who wouldn't make improvement lists, who weren't embarrassed by her.

It turned out not to be so easy to find another place. She even walked by Linden's table. It was full. Linden gave her a head tilt of acknowledgment. But she didn't clear a space for Nolie to sit. She probably figured she was going to sit with Jessa.

Nolie'd always had Jessa.

Who else was there?

Mindful Maddie. Even her table was full.

Finding a seat was getting urgent. Like when you really, really have to pee, and the teacher is in the middle of something and doesn't see you squirming in your seat waving your hand wildly.

Nolie had to find a place, ASAP. She was starting to attract attention. Like a lost child at the beach. A last desperate scan of the dining hall showed only one option: a square table with four seats and a girl sitting alone. A girl who always sat alone. Who'd made it clear that she didn't want to sit with anyone else.

Shady Serena.

Jessa had crowned her Shady. She said she was so quiet that she must have some big secret to hide.

But if Nolie couldn't bring herself to sit with Jessa, she had no other choice. She put her tray down across from Serena's.

Serena barely even looked up. She shifted back in her chair, as if she needed more distance from Nolie.

Serena looked the opposite of cool. She wore beat-up penny loafers and her kilt well below her knees. Not in the trendy way of a girl trying to make a fashion statement. It was just who she was. Like she wanted not to be noticed. And it worked.

Even Jessa had stopped noticing Serena after a couple of months.

They all had.

Until now. When Nolie sat through lunch with her and chewed her grilled cheese in blissful, beautiful silence.

There was another meaning to the word *shady*, Nolie realized. There was the meaning that Jessa intended—someone who was suspicious or deceptive. But shady could also be a good thing—like the shade of a tree, that sheltered you from the heat of the sun.

Maybe Serena's shadiness was the protective kind, that kept you safe and under cover.

Serena got up from the table as soon as she finished eating—what appeared to be a cucumber and cream cheese sandwich that she must've assembled from the salad bar—and left the dining hall without a word.

Sitting there for the last part of lunch by herself, Nolie no longer felt so protected, shaded. She felt exposed, like the fluorescent lights shone a spotlight on her, put her on a stage, all alone.

Apparently Jessa took Nolie not sitting with her at lunch as a major betrayal. Because that afternoon in chorus, Jessa stayed on the opposite end of the room from Nolie. She put all her attention on Calliope, acting like Nolie didn't exist.

Serena wasn't in chorus, which must mean she was in instruments. So Nolie found a place among a group of random girls who probably wondered why she wasn't with Jessa.

"We're going to sing one of my very favorites today," Ms. Cantwell said, clapping her hands together. "It's simple, to get us warmed up, and the song happens to be called *Simple Gifts*. Kind of a nice thought to keep in mind as the school year ramps up. First listen to the lyrics as I sing it to you, and then we'll sing together."

The tune was immediately catchy. Nolie'd heard it somewhere before, but she couldn't figure out where.

"All together now," Ms. Cantwell said, arcing her fingers over the piano. It was the kind of song that made you feel at peace as you sang it.

"I recognize it," Maddie said after they'd finished.

"It's a nineteenth-century Shaker song," Ms. Cantwell said. "The composer Aaron Copland used its melody for the score of the ballet *Appalachian Spring*. You might recognize it from that."

Ballet. Nolie couldn't escape from it. Everything always seemed to come back to ballet.

"Yeah, I think I have that on my meditation playlist," Maddie said.

Ms. Cantwell nodded. "Sections of it could be meditative, I suppose."

They spent the rest of class learning the second part of the song and then singing it in rounds. Because Nolie was sitting far enough away from Jessa, she didn't have to be in her group. She sang in her loudest, strongest voice. The rounds weren't supposed to be a competition, but still, she wanted her group's to be better.

At the end, as everyone gathered their things for their next classes, Ms. Cantwell flashed the lights on and off. "I have a special announcement," she called out. A wave of chatter started among the girls, guesses at what she was going to announce: the fall middle school musical.

"I'm overjoyed to share that our musical this fall is *Annie*! Which means we'll get one very special leading lady, but of course there are many wonderful parts to go around for everyone who's yearning for a turn onstage."

She went on to tell them about auditions and

rehearsal schedules, and all the other rules and expectations, but Nolie tuned out. *Annie* was one of her and Jessa's favorite movies to watch and sing together when they were younger. They'd dream of being orphans, which Linden made fun of them about. Jessa would sing Annie, and Nolie would take the parts of supporting roles as needed, from the dog Sandy to the orphans. And when Linden was around, and willing to join in, they could sometimes get her—or Andie, when they were at Jessa's—to play evil Miss Hannigan.

Now Nolie tried to catch Jessa's eye across the room. Surely this musical could bring them back together. With Jessa by her side, Nolie would try out for *Annie*. Even though she'd probably only get a minor role, it'd be fun.

But without Jessa, Nolie couldn't bring herself to do it. She'd feel too much like she was intruding on Jessa's territory. Theater was Jessa's thing, not Nolie's.

Jessa was an expert at ignoring what she didn't want to see. Nolie watched as she twisted her good-luck crystal and whispered to Calliope. Probably something about how they were going to try out together. She wished she had her seashell necklace to fidget with;

she picked at the dry skin on her thumb, instead.

In the locker hallway after school, Nolie searched out Jessa again. But Jessa was turned away, surrounded by Calliope and Vivian and the other girls who sat with them at lunch.

Snippets of their singing soared down the hall and prickled in Nolie's ear: *"The sun'll come out tomorrow . . . "*

Nolie could try to join in. She could belt out a loud, *"Bet your bottom dollar that tomorrow, there'll be sun!"* Her favorite line of the song. Show them that she could sing as loud as the next person.

But Jessa and the other girls had linked arms, forming a tight circle that kept Nolie out.

She could see where she wasn't wanted.

If Jessa was going to ignore her, Nolie would stay as far away as possible. For all Nolie cared, let Calliope play Annie's dog, Sandy. It suited her.

Maybe, Nolie realized, that's the kind of friend Jessa wanted. A friend who'd follow her and be unwaveringly faithful to her, like a dog. A dog that begged for the occasional treat as a reward. That wasn't who Nolie wanted to be.

Mom always liked to say, "Both things are true," when Nolie and Linden had a disagreement. There wasn't always just one answer to a disagreement. Both sides of an argument could be true and valid. Nolie'd thought she could figure out how to stay true to herself and be friends with Jessa at the same time. But it was beginning to feel like both those things couldn't be true. Like it was impossible to be herself *and* be friends with Jessa.

Maybe she did need help, after all. From the one person who always knew how to make things better.

Grandma.

7

THE COMPASS

"Come in, doll." Grandma greeted Nolie at her apartment door with a warm hug. "No playdates today?"

"Grandma, we don't do playdates in sixth grade."

They took seats at Grandma's polished wood dining room table. The table could magically fit twelve people for family dinners, but was also just the right size for two people to have an after-school snack of sliced apples and crackers and cheddar cheese, which Grandma set out on a plate for Nolie.

"So, what do you call it now? Hanging out? Chilling?"

"Oh my." Nolie slapped her palm to her forehead.

Even not-cool Nolie knew that Grandma was *so* not cool. She pronounced *chilling* like she was describing a step in a recipe.

"What about that friend of yours? Jessica? The one you're always with?"

"She's got other things," Nolie said. "And it's Jessa, short for Jessamine. But don't call her Jessamine, or she'll chew your head off."

"As you would when someone calls you Magnolia."

Nolie thought about how Dad said Grandma never liked that name. Was she trying to remind Nolie that Magnolia wasn't the right name for her? Did her name even matter, to Grandma?

"Kind of," Nolie said. She nibbled on an apple slice, and considered how to ask. "Except, what if I want to call myself that?"

"Magnolia?" Grandma blinked.

"Yeah."

"Why?" Grandma was an expert at feeling out what was really bothering Nolie before giving her opinion.

"It sounds more grown-up. Cooler. Or something. People always think that Nolie is a little boy's nickname."

"Do they really?"

Nolie shrugged. "Sometimes. They'll ask if it's short for Nolan."

"Hmm. I like the name Nolan. If you'd been a boy . . . "

"Grandma! Not funny. Besides, Dad told me you never even liked the name Magnolia?"

"Really?" she said, eyebrows raised. "He said that?"

"Can't you just answer a question without asking me another question!" Nolie tried to keep her voice calm. Sometimes she couldn't help getting frustrated with Grandma. She just wanted answers.

A smile turned up the corners of Grandma's mouth. "Remind me, what was the question?"

Nolie sighed. "I don't even know. It's about names, I guess. Whether I should start going by Magnolia. To sound more grown up." But it wasn't about names, not really. It was about Jessa, and who she wanted Nolie to be.

"In my opinion, call yourself whatever you want to be called. I'll love you no matter what your name is." Grandma tilted her head and paused before continuing. "You know, your great-great-grandfather, when he was in Odessa, his name was Haim."

"Wait, what? You mean Henry? The guy with the compass?"

"Yes, he came to this country as Haim Levy. He legally changed his name, and started over his new life here as Henry Levy. A respectable, American-sounding name. And he chose to name my father—his son—Joseph, instead of the Hebrew version he would've called him in Odessa. Yosef."

Nolie'd heard of people changing their names, like celebrities who had stage names, but she'd never thought it'd happened in her family. "So Joey's Shoes would've been Yosef's Shoes? Or is there a nickname, like Yosi's?"

Grandma laughed. "Maybe he'd have changed his name himself. Or made up the name for the store. Because, can you imagine Yosi's Shoes being the Upper West Side institution it is today?"

Nolie shook her head.

Grandma continued. "Same on Grandpa Leon's side." Nolie's Grandpa Leon, Dad's father, Grandma's husband, had died when she was three. All she remembered of Grandpa Leon was that he smoked cigarettes even though he knew it was bad for him. Or maybe Nolie just remembered that because it was one of the stories Grandma still told about him. She said she made him stick his head out the window to smoke, but the apartment still smelled of it, to her, after all these years. "His family name was Bechowitz. Your great-grandfather shortened it to Beck when they came here."

"So, I could be Magnolia Bechowitz?" How had Nolie never known this? She could've been an entirely different person.

"Exactly."

"And Linden would be Linden Bechowitz," Nolie mused, trying to wrap her head around it all.

"Then the world would definitely know our girl is a Jewish Marie."

Why was Grandma so fixated on Linden being a Jewish Marie? Linden was going to be Marie, whether she was Jewish or not. Her religion didn't seem to matter to anyone except Grandma. "What's the big deal, for people to know she's Jewish?"

Grandma took a deep breath. "Did I ever tell you how my first roommate in college had never met a

Jewish person in her life? She'd been raised to think that Jews had horns on their heads. She wanted to touch my head! To see if she could feel the horns. She was amazed to discover that I didn't have any. Can you imagine?"

Nolie shook her head. She couldn't imagine. There were so many Jewish people in New York City. A bunch of girls at school were. It's not like it was some big secret that she was Jewish, but it was also something that people didn't necessarily know about her, from her name or the way she looked.

It had happened just last year, in school. They were talking about Christmas and the holidays, and Nolie announced that she didn't celebrate Christmas because she was Jewish, and Elinor Fowler said in surprise, "You're Jewish?" In a weird way, that made being Jewish feel like something bad to Nolie. Not necessarily something to hide. But something about her that made her different.

She remembered when she was young, maybe four, and she noticed the word *Jewish* for the first time. It sounded like a funny word. She'd whispered it over and over again making the syllables into nonsense. *Jew,* sounded like a hard "you"—an accusation. And the *ish* threw the hardness to the wind. Like a breeze whistling through your lips. It'd made her laugh. And then, as she'd gotten older, *Jewish* had sometimes felt like a dirty word—something you didn't want to identify about yourself in public. At least, not in certain places. Places where you might be the only Jew.

Grandma continued. "Now, there's still plenty of antisemitism around. Hatred toward Jews. But, we're lucky to live in a time and place where we don't have to change our names or hide our identities. So I guess I want Linden to own it. To be proud that she can do something that she might not have been allowed to do in another place or time, because of her religion."

Nolie knew about antisemitism. How every year at Passover, they retold the story of their ancestors escaping slavery in Egypt. And the Holocaust, when nearly six million Jews in Europe were murdered. More recent attacks on synagogues. But it all seemed so far away. Not like something that would ever happen to her—not here. Not to them.

"I guess our family changing their names, it's like

Alicia Markova changing her name to fit in," Nolie said.

"Yes," Grandma nodded. "Exactly the same. It's called assimilation. When one culture changes their ways to fit in with the dominant culture. As a way to blend in, and advance themselves. To get ahead. Businesses wouldn't hire someone who had a Jewish-sounding last name. Clubs and colleges wouldn't let in too many Jews, if any at all. So they changed it."

That made Nolie think of her situation with Jessa. Of changing yourself to fit in with other people. Nolie took a deep breath, pausing to figure out how to word her next question. "If a friend wanted you to act a certain way, to change yourself, to fit into her idea of how she thinks you should be, and you did it, would that be assimilation?"

Grandma tapped her red-polished fingernails on the table. "That's a good analogy. It's definitely a similar idea. Changing how you act to fit in with a certain friend."

"But what if it's because the friend thinks it'll make you better? You know, to improve yourself?"

Grandma squinted as if to peer into Nolie's heart

and mind. "Do you feel like you need to change? Or is this some silly idea your friend has? I suppose it depends on whether the changes mesh with your soul. *Fitting in* is one thing—changing yourself so that people accept you. Like what our ancestors did to fit in when they emigrated here. But that's not true belonging. *Belonging* means being accepted for you. For who you are."

Nolie suddenly felt like the air in Grandma's dining room, which faced into an airshaft, was tight and stifling. Maybe, if she told Grandma exactly what the situation was with Jessa, then Grandma could give more specific advice.

But before Nolie could fill her in on the details, Grandma's phone rang. Nolie silently willed Grandma to ignore it, but Grandma looked at the screen. "It's your mom," she said, pressing the button to answer.

Nolie ran through her schedule in her head. It was only Monday. Was there somewhere she was supposed to be that she'd forgotten about? A dentist or doctor appointment? But she couldn't think of anything.

Mom's voice echoed through the phone. Something about Linden . . . stuck at work . . . helping out . . .

"Sure," Grandma said. "Yes, Nolie's here now. Of course. Five-thirty? I'll be there. And Nolie can stay? Wonderful. Terrific. Yes, I'll let her know."

Grandma set the phone down. "Mom asked if I could pick up Linden from ballet and give you girls dinner here tonight. Both she and Dad are running late at work."

Of course it was about Linden. It was always about Linden and her schedule and what she needed. Linden was in seventh grade. When were Mom and Dad finally going to tell her to grow up and get home from ballet herself? It's not like she was a toddler who needed to get picked up all the time. But Linden still wanted it. She loved the attention, making everyone go out of their way for her.

Nolie—she wasn't like that. She knew how to take care of herself, to be independent.

"Mom said I could stay here alone while you pick up Linden?"

"If that's what you prefer. Or we can have more time together? I figured we'd walk, get some fresh air? Continue our conversation?"

Nolie considered. She could use the time to tell

Grandma what was going on with Jessa, get her advice. But Mom's phone call had broken the moment. And Grandma had given her some ideas to think about. She could figure it out; she didn't need Grandma or Mom to help her all the time, how Linden did.

"I'll do my homework," she said.

So that's how Nolie found herself alone at Grandma's, sitting at the antique desk by the window in her living room, trying to focus on her math homework.

But she couldn't focus. Being alone in Grandma's apartment felt weird. There were sounds Nolie'd never heard before. The whir of the elevator cables and the *beep-beep-beep* of the elevator doors. The air-conditioning units that shuddered on and off every few minutes. And the cars honking and bus brakes screeching from busy Central Park West below.

Nolie got up from the desk and paced around the living room. Examining the books on the shelves, the photographs, the antiques, relaxed her.

She picked up the compass, the one that belonged to her great-great-grandfather. The one who'd changed his name from Haim to Henry. Who'd brought this compass with him from Odessa. He'd lived in Brooklyn and been a janitor or fruit seller or something. He'd done well enough to send Grandma's father, Joseph, to college, and help him start Joey's Shoes.

Nolie turned the compass in her hands, wondering about what it was like in Odessa, where he'd come from. Who'd she be if Haim/Henry had never left. And she wondered where the compass would go next.

Grandma enjoyed giving away her various treasures to her grandchildren. Sometimes they'd be at her apartment, and Grandma would get inspired. She'd decide a certain piece of her jewelry was just right for one of her granddaughters. Grandma tended to give necklaces to Linden, because she said she had the most elegant long neck to show it off. Earrings went to Anna because she was the only one with pierced ears. And Nolie got things like brooches and interesting objects, like a little porcelain bunny painted blue and gold.

Grandma had never mentioned giving away the compass, though Nolie'd always had her eye on it. Now, she held out the compass to let the arrow settle on north. A calm feeling washed over her. She got a solid, deep breath in for the first time, all day.

The sound of the elevator landing. Footsteps. Voices. Grandma and Linden. The front door opened.

Quick. Nolie slipped the compass into her backpack and slid back into the desk chair. She grasped her pencil, pretending to be hard at work on her math.

"I'm starving!" Linden announced, dropping her backpack and ballet duffel inside the front door. "Nolie! We ordered already. Chinese."

"Mr. Tang's?" Nolie asked, a sinking feeling in her stomach. She was still full from her snack.

"Yup. Steamed chicken and broccoli, extra sauce on the side. The way you like it," Linden said.

Nolie couldn't tell if Linden was being serious or not. But she didn't want to act immature and fight about it in front of Grandma, who was in the kitchen getting plates and silverware.

"I'm not even hungry," Nolie said.

"Too bad. You can eat leftovers later. Or tomorrow." Linden winced as she pulled her tight bun out of its hundred bobby pins and let her hair tumble down long and loose. Her hair was the same color as Nolie's, but so much thicker and bouncier and shinier. Linden preferred to wear hers down. It was as if her hair was a living thing that got confined and trapped by the tight buns she was forced to wear for ballet, and it couldn't wait to get free. Whereas Nolie felt more comfortable with her hair pulled back tight, out of her face, even though she didn't have to.

Linden looked down at her hands, to examine her fingernails which she spent way too much time filing and shaping to make up for not being able to wear polish or have pretty toenails. Nolie realized she'd picked away a whole patch of dry skin on her own thumb and it was looking raw and red. She curled it into her palm to hide it.

"So, *Annie,*" Linden said. "You going to try out?"

"Why would I?" Even as Nolie snapped back at Linden, she knew she was digging an even wider gap between her and Jessa.

"Why not? It's not like you have anything else to do."

Unlike me. Linden didn't even have to say it.

"It's not my thing."

"What're you talking about? All those times you and Jessa watched it on repeat? Driving me crazy with your screechy voices? C'mon, Noles, you know it by heart. I thought you'd be super excited."

"You thought wrong." Nolie crossed her arms. "Theater is Jessa's thing. Not mine."

Linden's face softened. "Is this about you and Jessa? I kind of noticed you weren't really hanging out."

"You did?" Nolie'd assumed Linden was too busy to notice.

"Maybe it's a good thing, you know? Like I was saying the other day. All the girls in my grade are kind of wondering what's up with her. I mean, she's acting like she wants to be in high school already. Seriously."

A line from the song they'd learned in chorus that day ran through Nolie's head: *'Tis a gift to come down where you ought to be . . .*

Linden knew exactly where she ought to be. Her whole life was scheduled, planned out, according to her classes and rehearsals for ballet and bat mitzvah prep. The stage was where she ought to be. She'd known it since she was four years old.

Nolie, on the other hand, had no idea where she should be. Lots of places felt right to her—Grandma's beach cottage and apartment. Home. Joey's Shoes. There were also places that used to feel right, but didn't anymore, like Jessa's apartment.

Maybe eleven was too young to know where you ought to be, but when other people seemed to know, to have an answer already, it was hard to be the only one who wasn't sure.

At least that night at Grandma's, her fortune cookie from Mr. Tang's wasn't empty. *Follow what calls you,* it said. But Nolie listened, and didn't hear anything calling her besides the chatter of Linden and Grandma talking about rehearsals and the never-ending *Nutcracker*.

Later, on their way home, after Mom came to pick them up, Nolie patted the outside pocket of her backpack where she'd stuck Grandma's compass. A compass was a tool that helped you to navigate. To find out where you ought to be. Right? Maybe that's why she'd taken it, instead of putting it back on Grandma's table.

She set her backpack down gingerly on the floor of their bedroom and pulled out the compass. She wasn't doing anything wrong, just borrowing it for a little while. If she'd asked, she bet Grandma would've let her. It was like she'd meant to ask, but had forgotten to.

She'd return it to Grandma's next time she was there.

Nolie didn't want anything to happen to the compass. So she placed it gently on the windowsill, behind her headboard. Alongside the seashell necklaces, her—and Linden's—other pieces of treasure from Grandma. She'd just keep it there, for a bit.

Safe and sound.

8

LIFE SAVERS

All the next day at school, Nolie felt unsettled about the compass. As much as she liked having it, part of her knew she shouldn't have taken it from Grandma's without asking. At the same time, it wasn't hurting anyone for her to keep it, temporarily. Until she navigated her way through whatever was going on with Jessa.

As far as she could tell, Jessa was most definitely ignoring her. She pretended not to see Nolie in the locker hall before homeroom. So Nolie didn't even think to sit with Jessa at lunch. She simply took her seat across from Serena. Again they ate in silence.

Nolie stared at Serena while she chewed her chicken fingers, challenging her to say something.

Finally, toward the end of lunch, after she'd finished eating, Serena looked up. "You okay?" she asked with concern on her face.

"Okay?" Nolie scoffed. Sure, she'd been trying to provoke Serena to talk, but why would Serena think she wasn't okay? "Yeah, why?"

"Um, nothing." Serena put her hands up to show that she'd meant no offense. "You were staring at me. Like you had something to say. Or something's wrong. You know." She shrugged.

"Sorry, I don't know." Nolie didn't mean to sound so defensive, but the last thing she wanted was for Serena to feel sorry for her.

"Okay, then. You're the one who chose to sit here. No one asked you to. I was just trying to be nice." Serena pushed her chair back from the table and lifted her tray to clear it.

Nolie wanted to shout back at her, to tell her that she was sitting there only because she had nowhere else. But she held it in. And then, as Serena walked away, Nolie felt an unexpected sense of loss. She wasn't trying to be friends with Serena, but now she was more alone than ever, isolating the one person who'd shown some kindness toward her.

In PE they had to run laps in the gym. Nolie sprinted to catch up with Jessa, but Jessa increased her pace to stay half a lap ahead. If Nolie slowed down, so did Jessa. If Nolie sped up, Jessa did, too.

Nolie was sweaty and out of breath for chorus, but she got there early, to take a spot near where Jessa had been the day before. Jessa came in, took one look at Nolie, and picked a spot on the opposite side of the room. Again.

Ms. Cantwell had everyone sing songs from *Annie*. Nolie tried to make eye contact with Jessa during "It's the Hard-Knock Life." Nolie made sure to stamp extra fiercely. Jessa *had* to look at her and laugh when they stomped their feet. But Jessa's willpower was stronger. She made Nolie feel like she'd been cast under a spell of invisibility.

Nolie couldn't face going home alone after school. Everyone else had activities to rush off to: tennis, piano lessons, dance, fencing. Everyone except for Nolie. She didn't want to go back to Grandma's until she was ready to return the compass, or she'd feel too guilty. She could go to Joey's, but couldn't imagine putting on her cheerful salesperson smile that day. A sudden feeling came over her—she wanted Mom. Which meant going to see Mom at work. Mr. Weiler's.

Mr. Weiler's building was about ten blocks from school, on Park Avenue on the Upper East Side. Nolie took her time getting there. She bought herself a chocolate milk and a bran muffin at a deli. She stopped in the neighborhood bookstore and read first chapters of various books until the bookseller gave her the *are you going to buy something, because this isn't a library* stare. She browsed the shelves of the gift store that sold the cutest, most overpriced erasers and pen sets. Nothing she'd be able to buy.

Finally, closer to the end of Mom's shift, she ambled over to Mr. Weiler's building. The doorman didn't bother to ring her up. He gave her the nod which meant he recognized her, and the button for Mr. Weiler's floor was already lit up when she got in the elevator. She pushed the front door open and stepped into the black-and-white marble-checked entryway.

Through the living room doors, Nolie got a glimpse of Mom tending to Mr. Weiler, fixing the sheets and blankets around him. He was in his hospital bed. The heart rate monitor next to him kept a steady beat.

Mom tiptoed out of the living room and shut the door behind her. "Nolie," she said in that warm but hushed voice she used at work. Nurses must take special voice training classes to teach them how to keep the right volume level. A level Nolie could never stick to. "Don't get all settled. I guess I forgot to tell you I finish a bit early today."

"Oh." Nolie dropped her heavy backpack to the floor anyway. Her metal water bottle clanged loudly on the marble floor. Mom winced and put her finger to her lips. Nolie started to step out of her sneakers.

"Keep your shoes on," Mom said. "I'm going to change. Tabitha's already here, getting ready."

Nolie saw Tabitha's wool cardigan—the one where she always kept a pack of cherry Life Savers in the pocket—draped over the bench in the entryway.

"I thought you finish at six?" Nolie asked. It was only five-thirty. She secretly hoped that it meant maybe she and Mom could do something special, the two of them. Convince Mom to buy her a rainbow pen set at the fancy gift store or walk through Central Park and really look at things, like the turtles in the pond. Not just rush through to get home.

"Last-minute change. Linden's rehearsal finishes early today. Who knows?" She threw up her hands as if it was all beyond her control. Which it was. Nolie knew that, but it didn't mean she had to accept it. "Give me a minute and we'll head out," Mom said.

Tabitha bustled in, ready to work in her nursing scrubs which had teddy bears printed all over. "Hello, sunshine." She blew Nolie a kiss, and pulled out her roll of Life Savers from the cardigan pocket and handed her one, like she always did.

"Thanks," Nolie said.

"How's school going so far?"

"It's okay." Nolie rolled the Life Saver around in her mouth, savoring the burst of cherry flavor. "The usual."

"Gosh, I remember when my kids were in middle school. It's tough, you know? Everything starts to change. But Linden seems to be doing well! Look at her, in *The Nutcracker*. Wow."

Tabitha beamed at Nolie, but Nolie couldn't match her enthusiasm. "Yeah, she's pretty impressed with herself."

Tabitha laughed. "I guess it's not so easy being the younger sister of the star. All that attention on her."

Nolie shrugged. She wished she had Grandma's seashell necklace to fidget with, but instead she picked at the raw patch of skin on her thumb, hoping Mom would hurry up and be ready.

"Tabitha," Mom called from the kitchen. "I meant to go over some notes on dosing with you."

So Nolie was left waiting in Mr. Weiler's fancy foyer with nothing to do but tune out Mom and Tabitha's chitchat about medicine schedules and—

"It's so great," Tabitha was saying, "to have that kind of passion at her age."

Why, oh why, did everything lead back to Linden? They certainly weren't talking about Nolie.

Nolie'd already finished the Life Saver that Tabitha had given her. And they were still talking.

About to melt from boredom, Nolie found herself reaching into the pocket of Tabitha's cardigan. To get one more Life Saver. One more to tide her over until Mom was ready to go.

But when she reached in, she saw the pack was nearly empty. There were only a few left.

For a second, she felt bad. She shouldn't take one—Tabitha probably counted on those Life Savers to get through her night shift. But then she noticed the other pocket—with a full, unopened pack of Life Savers. Tabitha had more than enough. She'd come prepared.

But just as Nolie picked up the nearly empty pack to pull out one more candy, Mom and Tabitha were back. Nolie had a split second to step away from Tabitha's cardigan—the Life Saver pack still in her hand.

She curled her fist tight around it and slipped it into the pocket of her hoodie as they said good-bye.

She wouldn't worry too much about Tabitha missing the end of this pack. If she even realized, she'd probably figure it fell out of her pocket somewhere, or that she'd forgotten she'd finished them.

Besides, a nearly empty pack of Life Savers was nothing.

In less than a minute, Mom and Nolie were back out on the street again in the evening bustle of Park Avenue.

No one looked at Nolie and thought, *That girl stole something.*

No one looked at her at all.

Only Nolie knew about the roll of candy in her pocket, pressed against her side on the bus ride to Lincoln Square to pick up Linden at ballet.

Mom had left more than enough time to get to ballet. Enough time for Nolie to try to do some homework in the waiting area. She pulled out a pencil and her copy of *The Odyssey*, for English, but it was hard to concentrate on underlining important words and phrases with all the parents chattering around her.

Especially the mom of Charlotte Fitzroy—the other Marie. Apparently, she was in the mood to compare notes with Mom about how anxious Linden and Charlotte might feel over the pressure of their roles.

"It's a lot, you know? They carry the whole weight of the performance," Mrs. Fitzroy said. "Charlotte's a strong kid—she has to be, of course, to have gotten the role. They both are. But to be onstage for the entire performance? Could you imagine doing that when you were their age?"

Mom sighed and stretched her legs. Her leather nursing clogs dangled off her toes, showing her thick wool socks, worn through in patches on the soles. (Nolie registered new socks for Mom as a potential Hannukah present.) Her legs looked like tree trunks compared to Mrs. Fitzroy's twiggy legs that ended in high heels. But Mom's legs were sturdy and strong. Legs that could easily lift and support another human body. Mrs. Fitzroy's legs looked like they might snap if she tried to lift anyone up.

"I couldn't have done it at any age," Mom said. "I don't know where Linden got her abilities from."

"I used to dream about dancing onstage when I was a kid," Mrs. Fitzroy said. "But I was nowhere near good enough. Not even for my small-town production. I stopped when I was ten. But Charlotte— she's something else. I mean, her figure, of course, is all mine." She gestured down at her skinny beanpole body. "But the talent, who knows? And the passion. You really need to have the passion for it."

That word again: *passion*. Nails on a chalkboard to Nolie's ears. It seemed like all adults cared about when it came to kids was their passions. Like they were My Little Ponies, and each kid should be marked with their own special power.

Mrs. Fitzroy turned to Nolie. "What's your thing, these days?" she asked.

Nolie's hands and teeth clenched. Her *thing* was that she didn't have a thing, and why would Mrs. Fitzroy care what her thing was, anyway? Sure, Linden was a superstar, but that didn't mean that Nolie was, too. She wanted to take her pencil and jab it into Mrs. Fitzroy's leg.

She searched her mind for something clever to say back. But all she could think of was what she'd taken. Grandma's compass. Tabitha's Life Savers. Even Linden's seashell necklace, if you wanted to get technical about it. But that wasn't the kind of answer Mrs. Fitzroy was looking for. Mom, too, was waiting— also curious to know how Nolie might answer.

Nolie wasn't going to lie. If she couldn't tell the full truth about what her thing actually was these days, then she'd at least not lie.

"I don't know. Nothing." She shrugged and looked at Mom for reassurance.

Mom didn't quite meet her eyes, but she leaned closer to Nolie and wrapped her arm protectively around her lower back.

"Nolie's my dreamer," she said. "She's got great ideas in her head." She gave Nolie a little squeeze.

Mrs. Fitzroy eked out a tight smile. "Not everyone finds their passion so early. Not like Linden and Charlotte. Oh, Charlotte mentioned that Linden might have to miss some rehearsals for her bat mitzvah?" Now Mrs. Fitzroy ducked her head toward Mom, as if to be totally confidential. "How's that going over with the directors, Linden missing rehearsals for a big party?"

Nolie felt Mom tense up as she uncrossed her legs and planted her clogs firmly on the floor. "I think they understand," Mom said, sitting up straighter, her voice icy, "that a bat mitzvah is more than just a big party. It's an important religious ceremony."

Mrs. Fitzroy pulled her head back in surprise and put her hand on Mom's arm. "You know I didn't mean anything by that. I just thought, well, you know, their expectations are so high around here. . . . "

Nolie managed to tune out her chatter for the rest of the wait, but the minutes ticked by painfully. She kept thinking about why Mom seemed so bothered by Mrs. Fitzroy's comment. It seemed kind of valid, to wonder whether the rehearsal directors would be okay with Linden missing some rehearsals. And how did Mom and Dad even decide which was more important, when there was a conflict with dates, between bat mitzvah prep and ballet?

At last the doors opened, releasing all the dancers in their tights and leotards into the waiting room.

Normally Linden and Charlotte would be arm in arm, gabbing and swooning about their mutual Marie love, how hard a certain step was to learn, their costumes or hairstyles or whatever. But that day, they exited as far apart as possible.

Linden looked over at Mom and Nolie like they were strangers there to pick her up, not her mom and sister. She kept walking, out the doors, onto the street, ahead of them.

Mom hurried behind her, leaving Nolie to lag. "What's wrong, Lindy? You okay?"

"I'm fine!" Linden said.

"You don't seem fine," Mom said.

"I don't want to talk about it!" she snapped.

Nolie looked back over her shoulder to see Charlotte whispering to her mother about something, watching Linden walk away. She was making big gestures with her hands like she had some important story to tell. Mrs. Fitzroy gave a look of alarm in return as Charlotte kept on talking.

Linden wouldn't speak the whole way home.

"What's wrong?" Mom kept asking from her middle seat between the girls in the taxi.

Linden refused to answer.

"I can tell when something's upsetting you."

Nolie cleared her throat, trying to signal Mom to keep her mouth shut, because Linden was getting more and more agitated.

But Mom kept poking at it. Trying to get an answer. Something she could help to solve, as if Linden were a patient that she could nurse into feeling better.

"Lindy, tell me. I'll listen and not say anything."

"Shut up! Please!" Linden exploded. Screaming it

so loud that even the driver slammed on his brakes, almost causing an accident. Nolie held on to her seat belt, clutched her backpack tight against her, for dear life. She looked out the window to see a driver next to them making angry gestures.

"Okay, then," Mom said. And not another word was spoken the rest of the way home. But Nolie could feel Mom's worry and Linden's fury, like the heat sizzling off the sidewalk on a hot summer day.

"You, come here now," Mom said to Linden when they got into their apartment.

"Mom, leave me—"

"No." Mom interrupted her. "We need to have a talk, alone."

Dad looked up from whatever he was reading on his computer. "Hello to you all," he said.

Linden practically growled in anger, but she followed Mom to her bedroom, where they closed the door.

"Everything okay?" he asked Nolie over the sound of muffled shouts (Linden's) and murmurs (Mom's) that spilled out from the hallway that led to the bedrooms. "What's the latest drama?"

Nolie shrugged. "Who knows?" If Linden wasn't busy being perfect and focusing on her ballet career, her moods alone soaked up all the air in the room. All Nolie could do was keep her head down and focus on her own problems, which no one else seemed to care about anyway. Linden's problems always required more attention, and were more interesting, than Nolie's.

Nolie went to her room and pulled out the pack of Life Savers. She popped one in her mouth. Only two more left. She considered putting the stub of the pack on the windowsill with the rest of her object collection, but Life Savers were too good to collect dust. She'd keep it in her backpack, for the next time she craved one.

That night, when they were in their beds, reading, and Linden had literally cooled off in the shower and the mood had diffused, Nolie tried to talk to her.

"What was that about—at ballet?" She held her book closed with a finger to keep her place.

"What?"

"I don't know, you seemed pretty angry. Something with Charlotte?"

"Oh, that."

For a second she didn't think Linden was going to answer. That she'd tell Nolie it was nothing, that she should stop being so nosy about every little thing.

But then she put down her book and turned to face Nolie. "You really want to know?" She curled into a tight ball, her knees pressed to her chest.

"Yes," Nolie said. But she held her breath and her heart pounded faster against her ribcage. Maybe she didn't really want to know. Not if it was something bad. Which it had to be, to make Linden so angry.

"It's Charlotte. She has this way about her. Of acting superior. Like she's such a better Marie. The rehearsal director used Charlotte as an example. For how I should be dancing. And I . . . " Linden rolled over to face the wall.

"Oh," Nolie said. Not sure what to say to comfort her sister.

"And then, I took a bathroom break when I was supposed to be doing some one-on-one work with my teacher. And I overheard some girls saying that ballet must not be that important to me if I had to miss it because of my big party."

"Don't they know a bat mitzvah is more than just a big party?" Nolie echoed what Mom had said to Mrs. Fitzroy earlier.

"Apparently not. I guess I'm the only one who has to miss a rehearsal for her bat mitzvah. And it's only, like, one rehearsal that I'm missing."

"So, big deal," Nolie said. If the girls didn't get the importance of a bat mitzvah, that was their problem.

"Yeah, but then, Charlotte was there, too. And she said something really awful. She said, 'I look more like a real Marie, anyway. Linden looks too Jewish.' And the other girls laughed."

Nolie felt a chill come over her. The same chill she felt when someone acted surprised to find out she was Jewish.

"What does that even mean?"

"I don't know. I stayed in the stall until they left. And then on our way out of rehearsal, I asked Charlotte. She said they were joking. That I shouldn't take it so seriously." Linden sucked in a deep breath and let it all out. "You happy now?"

Nolie wasn't happy. If anything, she was horrified. "That's awful."

"So maybe the last thing the world needs is a Jewish Marie." Linden's voice cracked.

Nolie wished she could find the words to comfort her sister, but all she could do was reassure her about how good she was. She'd been chosen, after all, for the part. She must be the best. "First of all, it's only been what, two days? You just started rehearsals! And, second of all, you're amazing. You're going to be the best Marie ever!"

Linden sat up straight in bed. "What're you talking about? That's totally beside the point. Brat. Making me tell you everything."

Linden threw her book across the room and turned off her reading lamp.

Silence.

Nolie's heart pounded. She hadn't mean to make Linden angry by asking about it. She'd wanted to be helpful.

"You should tell the teachers," Nolie whispered, hesitant. "It's like, totally antisemitic."

"No, it's not, and no, I shouldn't tell anyone. I

shouldn't have told you. It was a stupid comment. Forget I said anything."

But Nolie couldn't forget. She felt her sister's worry across the space between their beds even after she'd fallen fast asleep.

Nolie tossed and turned, flipping her pillow to find the cool side. Until both sides were hot. There was too much on her mind. The compass. Life Savers. Linden. Jessa . . . All of it whirled around and around in her head and made her heart pound faster.

She tried to take in deep, calming breaths, inhaling through her nose for three counts and out through her mouth, until her mind started to relax. At some point she must've fallen asleep. She had a nightmare that she was one of the mice in *The Nutcracker*, getting attacked by the prince and his soldiers. Not a ballerina dressed up in a mouse costume, but an actual, real live mouse. She felt herself scurry across a wooden stage, trying, trying to run away. But she couldn't escape the giant footsteps approaching to crush her.

When she woke up the next morning, she was

exhausted. She looked over to Linden, hopeful. Maybe she'd woken up in a better mood.

But Linden was still angry. She yanked and twisted her hair into a tight bun, chanting her Torah portion under her breath, and shoved her leotard and pointe shoes into her ballet duffel. She left early that morning, not waiting for Nolie to walk to school.

Nothing had changed.

9
NO LIE

Nolie sat with Serena at lunch every day the rest of that week. Aside from this new lunch companion, who was still pretty much silent, Nolie felt totally alone, like she'd lost both her big sister and her best friend at the same time. And she had no idea how she'd ever get either of them back.

But the following Monday morning, after a week of more or less ignoring each other, Jessa was waiting for Nolie at her locker. Surprise.

"Hi." Nolie tried to act like it wasn't odd that Jessa was standing there after they hadn't spoken in a week.

"Are you trying out for *Annie*?" Jessa asked.

Auditions were after school that day, but it wasn't really on Nolie's radar. Coming from Jessa, this felt like a trick question. "Are you?"

"I mean, it's kind of silly, but it'll be fun." Maybe Jessa had decided that *Annie* was silly as part of her big realization about wanting to be a serious stage actor.

"I still love it." Nolie wasn't ready to throw *Annie* under the bus yet. "But I'll leave the stage roles for the pros, like you."

Jessa narrowed her eyes. "Is that some kind of insult?"

"Huh? Why would you think that?"

"Why are you doing this, Magnolia?" The collar of Jessa's uniform polo shirt was turned up stiff around her neck. Both of the buttons were undone, and her amethyst crystal hung in the exact right spot to draw attention to her chest.

"Doing what?" Nolie asked.

"Don't pretend. You started sitting with Shady Serena, and now you're ignoring me."

That's not how Nolie'd seen things. All those days the week before, she'd tried to catch up to Jessa, to find a spot next to her. "Your table seemed kind of full."

"I'll squeeze in an extra chair for you. Come, sit with us today. You'll see."

After a week of ignoring her, why would Jessa suddenly want Nolie to sit with them at lunch? Maybe Jessa missed her, and wanted to go back to how things were. It was so tempting to slip back into their friendship. But Jessa only wanted Nolie around if she was going to try to be Magnolia. And Nolie didn't think that's who she wanted to be.

"I kind of like sitting with Serena. She's not so bad," Nolie found herself saying. Even though they'd barely talked, so she didn't really know that. For all she knew, Serena didn't even know her name.

What she did know was that Serena wasn't asking Nolie to try to be someone else. And that Serena's name suited her: she was calm, serene. Serena's quietness was like silent acceptance.

"We can't fit two extra seats at our table," Jessa said. "Whatever. Make your choice."

The homeroom bell rang, and Jessa didn't wait for Nolie to answer.

❋ ❋ ❋

At lunch Serena looked up from her table across the dining hall and gave Nolie an expectant smile. She hadn't started in on her sandwich yet. She was waiting for Nolie to sit with her.

Nolie'd noticed at homeroom how Serena had styled her hair like a little kid that day. It was pulled tightly in two braids, divided by a sharp part down the center of her head and a barrette on either side—red on one, yellow on the other. Combined with her blue-framed glasses, which she sometimes wore, sometimes didn't, it had the effect of making her look like a kindergartener learning the primary colors. Nolie saw some of the other girls shake their heads at Serena's style, or lack of it, but Serena herself didn't seem to notice, or mind, if she did.

Nolie floated between the tables and saw that Jessa's still had an empty seat that could be hers, if only she wanted it.

But if she didn't sit with Serena, no one would. Serena would go back to sitting alone again. Maybe she'd be disappointed for a little while, and then be okay with it. Or maybe, now that she'd had a taste of friendship, she'd never get over it. Either way, Nolie couldn't do that to her.

She tried to give Jessa an apologetic look as she passed her table, but she could bet that Jessa wouldn't understand.

Of course, Serena didn't even bother to say anything, least of all thank her, when Nolie sat down. She just smiled widely and swung her legs a bit, like an excited kindergartener. Nolie felt the warm glow of having done something to make someone else happy, but it was also mixed with the feeling that she'd made things worse between her and Jessa.

At the end of another quiet lunch, Nolie pulled out the almost finished roll of Life Savers that she'd taken from Tabitha.

Serena's face lit up.

Nolie could tell that Serena wanted one but wasn't going to ask. She held out the roll. "It's the last one. You can have it."

"Thanks," Serena said, taking the pack. "My favorite."

"Mine, too."

"My mom only lets us get the organic kind."

"They make organic Life Savers?"

"Apparently. Who knew?"

And then, in English that afternoon, Ms. Vazquez paired up Nolie and Serena to review each other's paragraphs on *The Odyssey*. "Serena, you go sit with Nolie," Ms. Vazquez said.

Serena moved her things to the desk next to Nolie, where Elinor Fowler had been sitting until she got moved to work with Calliope. Calliope's personalized pencil pouch was proudly displayed on her desk. Served her right to be stuck with Fowl Fowler, who'd admitted to wearing the same socks for a week straight last year when people complained of the stench in gym class.

"So, you know my name?" Nolie started.

"Huh?" Serena tilted her head, and took off her glasses. "Why wouldn't I?"

"I mean, it's not like we've ever really talked before."

"You've only been sitting with me at lunch every day and shared your candy with me. We've only been in the same school a whole year. Yeah, I know your name. I know the name of every girl in the middle school, in fact."

Nolie's eyes widened. Serena had a lot to say once she got going.

"Okay, then, just checking."

"You know what I like about your name?" Serena continued.

"What?"

"It means you're honest."

"How so?"

"*No lie*. I know it's pronounced No-lee. But if you break it down into syllables, that's what you get: No Lie."

Nolie laughed. She liked that. No Lie might be better than Magnificent Magnolia. But she wasn't sure that it was any more fitting a name for her. Could someone who'd taken things without asking claim not to lie? Nolie felt that unsettled tug-of-war inside of her again.

Maybe she was cunning, like the hero of *The Odyssey*. The ancient Greek hero Odysseus journeys home to his wife and son after the ten-year Trojan War, but it takes another ten years to make the voyage. He has all kinds of adventures and mishaps on the way. Odysseus and his men get shipwrecked, blown around by the gods, entrapped and tricked. And he tricks others, too, to escape. Like the one-eyed Cyclops. Odysseus tells him that his name is "Nobody Atall." So when the Cyclops' eye is speared by the men and he's wailing for help, and his friends ask him who hurt him, he cries out, "Nobody At-all!"

Their English paragraphs were about the meaning of home. They were supposed to imagine what it would be like to be away from home for an extended time. And what would define the essence of home, when you yearned for it like Odysseus.

Nolie worried that her paragraph was kind of boring. She'd started off by describing things matter-of-factly:

> In my home, I am the younger sister, which means that everything happens second for me. Which can be good, like when Linden convinces our parents to upgrade our electronics. That benefits me, too. But it can also be bad, like

when Linden gets new clothes and then hands the old ones down to me. The clothes that she chooses because they look good on her don't always look as good on me. Mostly, people think Linden is the more interesting sister because she's so talented and going to be a famous ballerina. Sometimes, it feels like there isn't enough room for me at home.

Nolie slid her paper across to Serena, who gave Nolie hers, which was a million times better:

Home is a four-letter word that evokes four million feelings. Home can be a happy place, when I come home at the end of the day to delicious smells from the kitchen while my dad cooks dinner. Home can be a sad place, when I overhear my mom and dad fighting, which they sometimes do, when they think I can't hear them. Home is a place that will always live inside of me. I will take it with me, wherever I go. Sometimes, I wish I could be like a hermit crab. Their shells are their homes. They carry their shells with them everywhere. But what's special is that they can take off their shells, and switch to a new one, when they outgrow the old one. Sometimes, I wish I could do that, too.

They looked up from reading each other's papers.

"That's really cool!" Nolie started. "Not the part about your parents fighting, I mean. The part about the hermit crabs. I didn't know that."

Serena's face lit up, like when she saw Nolie's Life Savers at lunch. "Yeah, you should watch a video about it. It's pretty neat."

"Have you seen it in real life?"

She nodded. "They live on beaches in tropical climates. So one time I was on vacation with my parents, and we found them on the beach. But I never saw them switching shells. I only saw that on a video." Then she leaned in closer, as if to say something top secret. "Did you know that they sell hermit crabs in pet stores?"

Nolie shook her head. She'd hardly ever spent time in a pet store. She didn't have any pets. Not even a fish. Mom said it was impossible because *she'd* be the one who'd end up having to take care of it and she didn't have the time or energy. Linden was too consumed with ballet to want a pet. And no one had ever bothered to ask Nolie.

"Good. Because that's the cruelest thing you can imagine. They're not meant to be kept in cages. In the wild they can live for more than thirty years. But in a cage, they'll die in under a year. And sometimes, pet stores will even paint their shells, which suffocates them to death. Slowly. And painfully."

Nolie felt a burst of outrage for those poor, captive, painted hermit crabs.

"And you know, even though they're called hermit crabs, they're not actually hermits? I mean, their shells are their homes, so technically, they live alone. But they're really social." She took in a deep breath, as if she'd forgotten to breathe while telling Nolie everything she knew about hermit crabs.

"Wow, cool." Nolie wished she had something to add.

"Ugh, you probably find this totally boring. Most people do." Serena slumped her shoulders, a bit crab-like herself.

"No, it's interesting. I just don't know anything about them."

"Do you like animals?" Serena asked, hopeful.

"Sure." Who didn't like animals?

"I love animals," Serena went on in a rush of words. "Not just in the way some people love their pets. But all animals, from hermit crabs, to sloths, to eagles, to elephants. That's why I have no friends at this school."

"I see," Nolie said, even though she didn't really. What did Serena's love of animals have to do with having no friends?

"My old school was really progressive. We could follow our own interests. So in third grade, I spent all my time researching hermit crabs during science class. It was so awesome. I just feel like the kids here, they don't think for themselves. You just have to follow what the teacher says, give them the answers they're looking for."

"Then why'd you come here?"

"Not because I wanted to," Serena said, twisting the bottom piece of one of her braids as she spoke. "Not because my dad wanted me to. It was all my mom's brilliant idea. She went here when she was a kid, and she thinks she's done really well in life. If going to a top college and having a big career that means you're too busy to see your kid is your idea of doing really well. She thought I wasn't learning anything at my old school. So that's why I'll never make any friends here. To prove her wrong."

"How is not making friends going to prove her wrong? Wouldn't not learning anything be a better way to make your point?"

"I'm the kind of person that can't help but do well in school." Serena shook her head, like it was a problem she didn't know how to solve. "I mean, I can totally not try, not even study, and I still get good grades. Don't kill me. I guess I'm wired that way. But making friends? That's a lot harder. With people—I mean. If I lived in a zoo, I'd be happy. Animals naturally like me.

And my mom doesn't just want me to learn. She also wants me to be *well-liked* and respected by my peers. Whatever."

Serena's mom sounded tough to please.

"So, if I was a zebra or something, we'd be friends?" Nolie asked.

Serena smiled. "Yeah, as long as I wasn't a lion."

"You don't strike me as the predatory type."

Serena laughed, a kind of braying sound, like a donkey. She covered her mouth with her hand to soften the noise. But Nolie liked her laugh because it was real—unlike Jessa's perfected, shrill giggle.

"Let's wrap it up. Five more minutes," Ms. Vazquez called from the front of the room. "I hope everyone's gotten some constructive feedback."

Nolie and Serena looked at each other and smiled.

"Did you even read mine?" Nolie asked. "Don't you need your glasses to read?"

"What, these?" Serena picked up the glasses like they were useless. "They're not prescription. Sometimes it's just nice to have a layer of something between me and the rest of the world."

Nolie liked that idea.

"And I did read your paragraph," Serena said.

"And?"

Serena put on her glasses. Maybe she needed a shield before she gave her honest opinion. "It's well written. But it doesn't give me a feeling for who you are, what home means to you. Except for in comparison to your sister. Put more of yourself into it."

Nolie tried not to let Serena's criticism pierce her heart. It was harsh. But probably true. She knew the paragraph didn't say much about her, but maybe that was her problem. What was there to say? How could she put more of herself into it when she didn't know who her self even was?

People were always going on about having a sense of yourself, as if it was something you could easily figure out, like a simple math equation. But Nolie didn't think it was as straightforward as all that.

Some people, like Linden, and maybe Serena, seemed to know themselves well. What they liked and didn't like, what they were passionate about, what was important to them. And others, like Jessa, were trying to change, to become who they wanted to be.

And then there was Nolie, who wasn't sure. About who she was, or who she wanted to become.

"Can I try on your glasses?" Nolie asked Serena, suddenly inspired. Maybe there was something to having a protective layer between you and the world.

"Um, sure." Serena slid them off and handed them over.

Immediately, Nolie didn't like the feel of having something plastic on her face, the weight of the frame on the bridge of her nose. And the glass lenses weren't totally clean. They were smudgy, making Serena look unformed, like a pancake flipped before it's ready.

"I think they need to be cleaned," Nolie said, handing them back to Serena.

Serena shrugged and blew on the lenses and rubbed away the fog with her shirt.

"Here, try them now," Serena said, holding them out.

Nolie shook her head. Fake glasses weren't for her. That's not what she needed.

That much, she knew.

* * *

You couldn't miss that *Annie* auditions were taking place that day after school. Snippets of song rang out through the hallways. Even Elinor Fowler got into the spirit, singing Miss Hannigan's song *Little girls, little girls, everywhere I turn I can see them* . . .

Jessa and Calliope were nowhere to be seen. Nolie would bet her bottom dollar that Jessa got to the auditorium early, to do her professional voice-training warm-ups before there were too many other girls around.

Nolie felt herself being pulled along by the flow of girls toward the auditorium. The entire middle school seemed to have turned out for a role, or to be a part of the backstage crew. Teachers were stationed outside the wide doors, checking the girls in and sending them to different sections depending on which roles they were interested in trying out for.

It would be so easy to follow the current, to let herself get funneled into one of those lines, and try for a part in the musical. Nolie could get a minor role, or be a crew member for set or costume design. There was a job or a role for everyone who wanted to participate. What was harder, somehow, was for Nolie to pull herself away.

She walked up as close as she could to the auditorium doors, to peek inside at what was happening. Ms. Cantwell paced on the stage, frantically checking her clipboard stuffed with sheets of paper. The other staff members of the music and performing arts departments looked harried, corraling the girls.

And then Nolie spotted the backs of two familiar heads leaning in close together, in the row of seats front and center. She'd know the back of one of those heads anywhere: Jessa. Which was confirmed when Jessa must've felt herself being watched and she turned slightly in her seat to glance back toward the door.

Nolie felt the urge to duck and hide. She was worried she'd been caught spying, but there was no way Jessa could identify her through all the crowds between them.

She peeked back in, and saw Jessa facing forward again, squeezing Calliope's hand, for encouragement or to get out her nerves or something.

All Nolie knew was that just a few months ago, it

would've been *her* whose hand Jessa was squeezing. She'd have been the one sitting next to Jessa, calming her nerves, reassuring her that she'd do great and get cast as Annie.

But now, it wasn't Nolie.

Not any longer.

It was like Nolie and Calliope were hermit crabs who'd traded shells.

10

LUCK AND LADYBUGS

After being paired together for their English paragraphs, Nolie and Serena started talking more at lunch. Maybe they were even becoming friends. It felt good to have a new friend, after so many years of being focused only on Jessa.

Still, it was a relief when the weekend finally arrived, and Nolie didn't have to worry about friend stuff.

Until Saturday morning.

Mom dropped off Linden at *Nutcracker* rehearsal and then went to an exercise class and to get her hair cut. The things she didn't get to do during the week.

Nolie and Dad got bagels—sesame with cream cheese and lox for him, cinnamon raisin with butter for her—and went for a walk around the Great Lawn in Central Park.

They stopped at the grassy area by the turtle pond, across from Belvedere Castle, and perched on the rocks to eat their bagels. It was one of those fall days when the temperature was just right: you could wear short sleeves and feel deliciously warm in the sun, but not too hot, with a hint of cooler weather to come. A freshness in the air, a sign of change.

Nolie didn't always love the hustle of living in New York City, but in certain moments like these, sitting in the park with the tall buildings surrounding them, she felt like a character in a storybook.

After, Dad wanted to stop by Joey's, but Nolie wasn't in the mood. She considered going to Grandma's but was still avoiding that while she had the compass.

Nolie went home and settled on the couch to watch a reality show about people going on adventures around the world. A few episodes later, a text message pinged, from Jessa: *Hiya. I know things r weird. Sorry. Dunno. Do u really want 2 hang w*

Shady Serena insted of me? Miss u. Xoxoxoxoxoxo

That brought a little smile to Nolie's face—the last part about Jessa missing her and all the hugs and kisses.

Not the part about Shady Serena.

Because Serena wasn't so shady after all. Not since Nolie'd shared her cherry Life Savers and she'd told Nolie about hermit crabs and they'd read each other's paragraphs and they'd started to talk at lunch.

Turned out, Serena was kind of interesting. She had a lot more to say than just about hermit crabs. She told Nolie other things about animals, like how a group of parrots is a pandemonium, and a group of ladybugs is a loveliness. And some people believe ladybugs bring you luck. If a ladybug lands on you, count the number of spots to predict how many years of good luck you'll have. The redder the ladybug, the better your luck will be.

Serena had a guinea pig named Wilbur and a betta fish named Harriet, but no dog or cat because her parents wouldn't let her. But she was working on them to adopt a shelter dog, as soon as they decided she was old enough to walk it on her own. She kept a list of potential dog's names for when she did get one. Right now Bingo was her top choice, but that'd surely change before she finally got a dog. She said Nolie had to come over and meet her pets some day.

Nolie could tell Jessa that Serena wasn't so shady, but Jessa wouldn't care about any of those things. And it wasn't the type of thing Nolie could explain about Serena anyway. Jessa'd have to learn it from Serena herself, if she ever gave Serena a chance.

Or if Serena gave Jessa a chance, for that matter. They were complete opposites.

So Nolie wasn't sure what to write back to Jessa. How to say she missed her but didn't like that she was mean about Serena. She decided to think about it, let it settle in, and reply when the right answer came to her.

Mom and Linden came home from rehearsal later that day. A stony silence hung like a storm cloud over them. The kind that meant they'd had it out over something or other, and now weren't talking, for the sake of keeping the peace.

Linden stomped straight to their room and slammed the door, without taking off her sneakers, in defiance of their strict no-shoes-indoors policy.

Mom gave a long sigh as she stepped out of her flats and set her bag by the door. Dad opened his arms to pull her into a hug.

"I'm exhausted," Mom mumbled into his shoulder. "Her attitude. It's out of control."

"What happened this time?" Dad asked. "You didn't do her bun tight enough? She didn't pack the right leotard?"

"None of that. She won't even tell me what." Mom shook her head, and then looked at Nolie as if noticing her for the first time. She curled deeper over *The Odyssey* and pretended to be so absorbed that they'd keep talking in front of her.

No such luck.

"Oh, Nolie," Mom said, as if it was a relief to see her. "How was your day?" There was weariness in her voice that told Nolie that if she added anything more to her problems, it'd put her over the edge. She better be fine.

So that's what Nolie said. "Fine. It was fine."

Because *fine* wasn't exactly a lie. *Fine* didn't mean good, or bad. It meant that it just was. It'd happened.

Nothing much to report aside from Jessa's text, which hardly seemed newsworthy. Especially not in comparison to whatever Linden's drama was.

Later, after Nolie slipped into their room, she asked Linden what had happened. Maybe some more drama with Charlotte. Like the other day.

Linden looked up from where she was stretching on the floor. Nolie could tell from her expression that she wanted to yell at Nolie to get out and close the door behind her. But she didn't.

She huffed and angled herself toward the wall instead.

"You okay?" Nolie tried again, as she undressed and put on her pajamas.

"Tired," Linden mumbled. "It's a lot of work."

"Must be," Nolie said. Though she had no idea what "a lot of work" really felt like, and they both knew that. "But it's still fun, isn't it?" Maybe, if Nolie could get Linden talking about how great it was to be Marie, to star in the ballet, which had been her favorite thing in the world to talk about, she'd brighten up.

"Eh," was all she said. "I don't want to talk."

Nolie couldn't argue with that. Linden had basically told her to mind her own business. So that's what she'd try to do.

Somehow, Nolie forgot to write back to Jessa. She didn't remember until Monday morning, when they saw each other in the locker hallway.

Nolie's heart pitter-pattered, knowing how angry Jessa would be. In the whole history of their friendship, Jessa'd never been the first to apologize. And now she had, and Nolie had ignored it. By accident. Not that Jessa would accept that as an excuse.

Nolie approached her, but when Jessa spotted Nolie, she turned her back and opened her locker, rearranging the things inside.

"I'm sorry, Jessa," Nolie said. "I saw your text, and I meant to write back, but you know"—and here she lowered her voice, as if she was letting Jessa in on a big secret—"Linden was having all this drama, and—"

"C'mon, Magnolia, don't make up excuses," Jessa said, facing into her locker. "This isn't about your sister. You're ditching me for your other friend, who you know is kind of shady."

Nolie's blood started to boil. How was Jessa turning this into Nolie ditching her, when she was the one who'd found other friends and was trying to make her be different?

"Okay, you're right. It's not about Linden. It's just that, I wanted to write back, but I didn't know what to say. Because, the truth is, Serena's actually nice."

The homeroom bell buzzed.

"Look, if you really cared, you'd have replied." Jessa slipped her amethyst crystal off her neck and placed it on the shelf in her locker.

"What are you doing?" Nolie asked. Jessa never took the crystal off except for when she showered. Not even when she slept.

"Do you really want to know?" Jessa shook her head and stared into the distance. "Someone complained that my fidgeting with it was distracting them. I don't know who. But now I'm not allowed to wear it during class. Great. Just great."

She narrowed her eyes at Nolie, like maybe she was a suspect.

"Gosh, that sucks," Nolie said. It really did.

"Like you care." Jessa wheeled around, using her

elbow to slam her locker door shut, and stomped off to homeroom before Nolie could get in another word.

The only thing was, Jessa's locker door didn't stay shut. The metal clanged and swung back open.

Nolie went to close it for her. Of course she was going to close it for her.

But then she let herself take a closer look at the photographs Jessa had put up inside the door. And she counted—there were only two pictures of Jessa and Nolie. From when they were in second and third grade. Only two pictures, out of twelve. There were also two of Calliope, and one of her with Vivian and Calliope, together. Didn't Nolie deserve to have more pictures there than Calliope, given how much longer they'd been friends? She didn't even know who the other people were. Maybe girls from her theater program in LA.

Just as Nolie was about to close the door, she noticed the black satin cord of Jessa's necklace hanging over the edge of the shelf. Maybe that's why the door had bounced open to begin with.

Nolie went to push the necklace back in so it wouldn't get caught again. But a jolt of something ran through her as she felt the crystal in her fingers.

Luck.

Jessa always said that the crystal brought her good luck. Maybe that's what Nolie needed in her life.

Or, maybe, Nolie wanted something of Jessa's. A way to hold on to her, even as they were splitting apart.

She wrapped the crystal tight in her fist. The sharp point of it pressed into her skin. Nolie looked both ways to make sure no one was there, and slipped the necklace into the pocket of her backpack. She closed the locker door, double-checking to make sure it was secure.

But as she turned to walk to her homeroom, already late, who was there watching her but Calliope, like she'd appeared out of thin air.

So much for good luck.

It felt like that scene in *The Sound of Music*, near the end, when the Von Trapp family is hiding from the Nazis in the abbey. Nolie'd watched so many times and knew exactly how it would turn out, but still, she always panicked watching that scene, tensed in fear, holding her breath along with them. That's how she felt under Calliope's accusing stare. But she pulled herself together, threw back her shoulders, and lifted her chin.

"Oh, hi," Nolie said, all casual.

"What're you doing?" Calliope asked.

"Closing Jessa's locker. She left it open by mistake."

Calliope looked at Nolie's hands like she knew she was hiding something.

But she couldn't possibly know.

Nolie was certain Calliope hadn't been there when she put the crystal into her backpack.

She waved her empty hands at Calliope like she was saying a dramatic good-bye. "Off to homeroom!"

Jessa's crystal burned in Nolie's backpack all morning. She felt its power seeping into her, bringing her strength.

It was definitely good luck when Nolie and Serena got assigned to do a project together for social studies. A project connected to their English paragraphs on the meaning of home.

Mr. Reilly read out the list of partner pairings, and then explained the project to them. "First, spend some time reflecting on your own. Think about what *home* means to you," Mr. Reilly said. "You could take it in a literal sense—the physical space and surroundings of the place where you live. But you could also consider home as an abstract concept. What does the idea of a *home* even mean? On a societal level? Could *home* be defined by people, a society, or a religion—some individual or group that makes you feel like you belong? Or look at it from a scientific perspective—different animals and their habitats."

Serena waved her hand in the air excitedly.

"Yes, Serena?"

"So does that mean we can write about animals, instead of people?"

Calliope smirked at that, but Nolie felt defensive on Serena's behalf. "What's so funny?" she whispered to Calliope, channeling strength from the crystal in her backpack. Calliope sneered at her, and apparently Mr. Reilly heard her, too. He cast a *be quiet* look at Nolie before answering Serena's question.

"Yes, you can write about animals, but I want you to start from a place of self-reflection. Start from yourself, and your own idea of home, and see where that takes you. If that takes you to animals, then go with it. Any other questions?"

Elinor Fowler raised her hand and started speaking before Mr. Reilly called on her. "Do we have to work with partners? I mean, what if we have totally different ideas about what home means?"

Nolie wished Elinor hadn't asked that. She was excited to work with Serena, because she knew Serena would be full of ideas to help them get started.

Mr. Reilly smiled. "Thanks, Elinor. That question feeds perfectly into what I'm about to say. I actually hope you and your partner have different ideas about home. This is meant to be a dialogue, as much as an internal reflection.

"So, once you've had some time to come up with your own ideas about what home means to you, begin to collaborate with your partner. Have a planning session where you share your ideas, and brainstorm. Come up with a list of ways to present your ideas to the class. Successful presentations will include more than a straightforward report of your findings. Some creative ideas include writing and reciting poems, acting out a scene, slideshow presentations, dioramas, or other art projects."

Serena caught Nolie's eye across the room and gave her a double thumbs up. This was going to be good.

Nolie's good luck continued at lunch. Jessa ignored Nolie, as usual, which meant she hadn't realized yet that the necklace was missing. And Serena was full of enthusiasm for the social studies project.

"It's like the kind of thing we did at my old school," Serena said. "We can explore some ideas together. Places around the city that feel like home to us."

Nolie let Serena's excitement wash over her, and she kind of nodded and agreed to whatever Serena was saying, but didn't really contribute to the conversation. She couldn't figure out what was bothering her, until her walk home alone that afternoon.

When she thought of home, the first thing that popped into her head was how Linden was acting. It had all started with Linden throwing out the seashell necklace, like she no longer wanted to be a part of Grandma's tradition. And how it'd gotten worse since school started, and she'd been cast as Marie. And there was nothing Nolie could say about it, because all Mom and Dad cared about was supporting Linden and her passion.

But Serena suggested they explore different places, like it didn't have to be about their actual homes. Lots of places felt like home to Nolie. Obvious ones like Grandma's beach cottage and apartment, and Joey's. But more abstract ideas, too, like Mr. Reilly suggested. Religion—being Jewish. But while being Jewish was important to Nolie, she wasn't sure if it was the main thing that mattered to her. She couldn't think of only one thing, and she was pretty sure it would change over time.

It all came back to hermit crabs, again. How they could move to a new shell when they'd outgrown the old one. People, too, could outgrow one place or identity that felt like home and trade it for another.

Same with friendships. You could take off the shell of one friendship and move into the shell of another one. Maybe one shell didn't fit you for your whole life. Not when you had different sides of you to explore.

Like Jessa's nicknames for people, which gave them one defining adjective: Mindful Maddie, Shady Serena, Fowl Fowler, Magnificent Magnolia, Lucky Linden.

Those names were an easy way to explain people.

But most people couldn't be explained by just one adjective. There wasn't always one answer for anything. There was usually another side to every story, every description, every action.

And just as Nolie reached her building, a true miracle happened. A ladybug flew down, and landed on her arm! She smiled; it felt like a sign sent from Serena. She turned over her hand to cradle the ladybug in her palm and count the spots. Six. Not the most ever, but that was a pretty decent amount of good luck to get her started.

The words to a chant they used to say came into her head: *Ladybug, ladybug, fly away home* . . . Nolie couldn't remember the rest of it, but the ladybug seemed to get the signal. It spread its tiny wings and took off, and in the blink of an eye, it was gone.

That night, after Linden was asleep and Nolie was ready for bed, Nolie took out Jessa's necklace and held it up. She dangled it by the cord so her reading light shone through it, casting a prism on the wall. She tried to hypnotize herself with the crystal, to meditate

on it. To calm all the thoughts about Linden and Jessa
and home running through her head.

A sharp bark outside the window from a dog on
the street startled her. Nolie dropped the crystal to the
wood floor with a sharp *plunk*. Her heart skipped a
beat, afraid it had broken.

"What was that?" Linden asked, sitting up
suddenly. Still half asleep.

"Just, um, a coin," Nolie said. "Sorry."

Linden fell back into her deep sleep. In the
morning she probably wouldn't even remember that
she'd woken up.

Nolie scooped up the crystal from where it had
bounced under her bed and inspected it for damage.
No cracks or scratches—nothing. As solid as ever.

She should put it in her backpack. Bring it into
school tomorrow. Return it to Jessa.

But she wasn't ready. Not yet. Like with Grandma's
compass. She wanted to keep it for herself for a bit.

She placed the crystal necklace on her windowsill
behind her bed. Next to the compass and seashell
necklaces.

She knew these weren't things that really belonged

to her. That she'd have to give them back. But still, they felt oddly reassuring. Like she was building up her own collection of things that mattered.

Who needed ladybugs when she had Jessa's crystal and Grandma's compass to bring her luck?

11

STOLEN & WANTED!

Nolie didn't even have a chance to give back Jessa's necklace. Because the very next day, she came into school to discover that she was accused of being a criminal. Well—not her, specifically, but someone.

Jessa had handwritten signs and copied them onto neon lavender paper. Calliope was helping her tape them all over the middle school corridors:

Stolen & Wanted! An amathyst crystal necklace belonging to Jessa in class 6-F. Of great sentimentel value. A reward will be given to the person who finds and returns it. No questions asked.

Nolie ignored the spelling mistakes, but a ball of worry lodged in her stomach.

How could she give back the necklace now? It would be too much of a coincidence if she was the one who "found" and returned it.

Not that she could even return it today, because she'd left it on her bedroom windowsill. How could she explain to Jessa that she'd found the necklace and took it home with her?

At the same time, she couldn't not say anything. She couldn't pretend to miss those neon lavender signs screaming in her face like stop signs.

All through homeroom, Nolie fretted over her options.

Either, 1) she'd have to say something today, own up to having taken it home, and invent a good excuse for why.

Or, 2) she'd have to keep her mouth shut, pretend to have nothing to do with it, and then find a way to slip it back into Jessa's locker—or drop it in the lost and found box in the principal's office—without ever admitting to what she'd done.

Or, 3) not say anything today, but bring the

crystal into school tomorrow, and claim to find it then. That option appealed the teeniest bit, because Jessa probably had a good reward in mind. Plus, Nolie would be the hero for finding the crystal. Maybe even get in Jessa's favor again—

She cut that thought out of her head as soon as it entered. Because that wasn't her goal, was it? To get Jessa to like her again? Who even had to do that with a real best friend? A real best friend wasn't mean the way Jessa had been. A real best friend didn't judge who you were and try to change you. They accepted you, or they didn't deserve the title of best friend.

Option 1 would include lying to Jessa's face, making up a reason why she took the necklace home. Nolie was not a good liar.

That left Nolie with option 2, to keep quiet and find a way to slip the necklace back to Jessa.

But in the end, while she circled around her options in her head all day and jumped in panic every time someone called her name, she didn't have a choice. Jessa caught up with her just outside school and confronted her directly.

"You took it, didn't you?" she said, hands on her hips, as she walked with Nolie along the street toward Madison Avenue.

"What?" Nolie shivered, and pulled her hands inside her sleeves. She felt cold, suddenly, even though the temperature was still warm for the end of September, and the sun shone down brightly.

"You know exactly what I mean, Magnolia!" Jessa huffed a sigh of frustration. "Calliope told me. She said she caught you in my locker yesterday."

Nolie felt other girls look at them strangely as they walked past. She leaned in closer to Jessa, and kept her voice low. "I told her: your locker was open, so I did you a favor and closed it for you." She crossed her fingers. It was not a lie. Not exactly.

Jessa stopped short and grabbed Nolie's arm. "Look me in the eyes, Noles. Really. Look."

The sound of *Noles* in Jessa's voice got to her. Maybe underneath whoever Jessa was trying to be these days, the real Jessa, her forever best friend Jessa, was still there.

Looking in Jessa's eyes directly was harder than it sounded. Literally. Her eyes were so dark brown that the pupils blended, and you couldn't always tell which way she was looking. But at that moment, it was totally clear. She was looking right at Nolie. Down at her from her new height. They'd always been almost the same height, but at some point, without Nolie realizing it was happening, Jessa'd grown a few inches taller.

She jutted out her chin at Nolie and crossed her arms. "Now, tell me. Did you take my crystal?"

The right thing to do would be to admit it. To tell Jessa she'd taken it and meant to give it back. But there was no way Nolie could bring herself to do that. Yet she didn't want to lie, either. There had to be an in-between. Some way of saving herself. Of not lying, but not exactly telling the truth.

She stumbled over her words, searching. "I—um—I . . . "

"You, um, what? You know what we call you now, since you started hanging out with Shady Serena? *Nothing Nolie.* That's what. You're going to be nothing, if you don't give my necklace back." Jessa's dark eyes were cold and flinty, like they'd been that day at her house before school started.

But that mean look, and those mean words, didn't have the intended effect. They didn't suck the wind out of Nolie and make her want to beg for Jessa's forgiveness. Instead, they made her think that someone so mean deserved to have her favorite necklace, her good luck charm, stolen.

"I'm sure you'll find your necklace," Nolie said, feeling very dignified.

"Give it back, and we can forget this whole thing ever happened." Jessa clenched her fists at her sides. "I won't tell anyone it was you."

"What's the reward, anyway?"

Jessa snorted. "Is that what this is about for you, Magnolia? Getting something? You always want what other people have, don't you?"

Nolie wasn't sure what that meant. It was Jessa who wanted to change, to be different. But—was that why Nolie had taken all the things that belonged to other people? Was it about wanting what other people had? She shook her head.

Jessa continued her rant: "You act like you don't care about anything, but I know you wish you could be as amazing as Linden. I bet you're jealous of all the attention she gets. Which makes sense. I'd feel bad about myself, too, if I had an older sister like her. I tried to help you. I had a whole plan, and everything. But you're not making any kind of effort."

Nolie felt the same surge of anger she'd had when Dad tried to make her order Chinese food Linden's way. The anger that started when Linden cut Cousins Week short. She squeezed her fists so tight that her fingernails dug into the palms of her hands.

Nolie and Jessa used to joke that they knew each other better than they knew themselves. Like when they went to the movies, and Jessa would offer to get Milk Duds, because she knew that's the candy Nolie wanted. And Nolie would say she was fine with popcorn because that's what Jessa preferred. They'd end up getting both and mix handfuls of salty and sweet together. It was always so much better that way.

But this person standing before her—*this* Jessa—didn't know Nolie so well anymore. Sure, Nolie couldn't stand that their whole lives revolved around Linden and ballet, but that didn't mean she wanted to be like Linden. Jessa had it all wrong, if that's what she thought.

"I don't want to be your improvement project,"

Nolie managed to say. "And my name is not Magnolia."

Jessa shook her head. "Just give me back the necklace. Okay? That's all I want. My *grandmother* gave it to me." And she stomped away, leaving Nolie with that thought.

Because Nolie did understand the importance of a gift from a grandma. She had all the Cousins Week treasures from Grandma. The little gifts Grandma had given her over the years. And the compass, which Grandma didn't know she had, but still. She didn't even want to think about how upset she'd be if someone took one of those treasures from her. Or what it would be like, someday, when Grandma was no longer there.

"Someone stole Jessa's crystal. Can you believe it?" Linden had to go ahead and bring it up over dinner that night. Taco Tuesday, one of the few meals that Mom and Dad managed to pull together most weeks, because there wasn't much cooking involved and Linden's rehearsal didn't run too late on Tuesdays.

"Stole it?" Mom cocked her head in confusion, holding out the hard-shell taco she'd stuffed with chicken and cheese.

"Yeah, she put up these signs all over school," Linden continued in between bites. She didn't have any taco on her plate—just fillings. Lots of shredded lettuce and tomato and beans.

"Did you see that too, Nolie?" Mom asked.

"Couldn't miss it," Nolie grumbled, taking a large bite of her soft taco filled with guacamole and extra cheese.

"How does she know someone stole it?" Dad asked. "Maybe she lost it. Jessa's not always the most responsible. Every time she sleeps here, she leaves something else behind. We could have a whole box devoted to Jessa's lost and found."

Not these days. But no one else commented on how Jessa hadn't even been over to their apartment since the school year had started.

"Jessa said she's sure of it," Linden said.

Nolie tilted her head. How did Linden know so much about the situation? It felt like Linden was accusing Nolie as she spoke.

"She said the last time she saw it, it was in her locker," Linden continued.

"Geez," Dad said. "A thief! A mystery to be solved."

"I wonder if they can check the security cameras?" Mom asked.

Guacamole got stuck in Nolie's throat. She hadn't considered that.

"How would someone break into her locker, anyway?" Nolie said. "I bet she just lost it."

"How would you know?" Linden asked, homing in on Nolie now. "I never see you hanging out with her these days."

Nolie took a big gulp of water. This was *not* something she wanted to discuss with her entire family over Taco Tuesday. It was none of their business.

"Did something happen?" Mom asked, alarm spreading across her face. "We haven't seen Jessa over much. In fact, I don't think we've seen her since before the summer vacation."

"You haven't," Nolie said, grabbing for an excuse to cover with, quickly. "She's been super busy. With theater. She tried out for the middle school musical."

"Oh, we haven't heard about that yet." Mom sounded hopeful. "Which musical this year?"

"*Annie*," Linden said. And then, with a sly smile, "Remember how Nolie and Jessa were obsessed?"

"One of our favorites!" Dad said. "What part are you going to play, Nolie?"

"I'm not playing any part." Nolie glared at Linden, trying to get her to drop it.

"Why not? You and Jessa love singing those songs together," Mom said.

"It's not like kindergarten where everyone gets a part. You have to audition."

"So? You'd be great at it. *'Bet your bottom dollar . . . there'll be sun . . . !"* Dad broke out totally off-key.

Nolie covered her ears. Linden smirked, leaning back in her chair, arms crossed, like she was a judge presiding over the trial of Nolie: official sixth-grade outcast.

"Dad, stop!" Nolie yelled. "The auditions already happened and I didn't try out and I—I hate it, okay?! I hate everything!"

Nolie felt bad as soon as she yelled and took in the hurt, bewildered look on Dad's face.

"Nolie, what's gotten into you?" Mom said, shocked. The only one who didn't seem surprised was Linden. Like she'd provoked Nolie to yell because she knew something more. Something she wasn't saying.

Nolie got up from the table, leaving her half-eaten taco behind, and ran to their room. She slammed the door, chest heaving. Then, she checked the windowsill.

The crystal was still there. Along with the other things.

Linden didn't know anything. She'd just been needling Nolie, goading her. For fun.

Like it was a sport for an older sister to provoke her younger sister, for no reason.

She threw herself onto her bed, burying her face in her pillow as tears of shame and anger spilled down her cheeks.

There was a soft knock on the door. "It's me," Dad said. "Can I come in?"

"Sure." Nolie sniffled and wiped her tears with the edge of her blanket. But she couldn't look up at Dad as he sat down on the bed next to her.

"What's up with you, Noles?" Dad asked, rubbing her back.

"Nothing. I'm fine."

"Hey, stop." He placed his hand on her thumb, where she'd been picking at the skin.

All she wanted was for him to leave her alone. To

let her pick her thumb and wallow in her unhappiness.

"Is this about something to do with Jessa?" he asked.

Nolie shook her head. There was no way to explain anything to him.

"Do you want to talk to Mom, instead?" Nolie knew that sometimes Dad thought his daughters had "girl issues" which only Mom could help with, and that just made her even more annoyed.

"Seriously, Dad, I'm fine. Okay? I'm just . . . tired." That's what everyone else always said when they didn't want to talk, when they wanted to be left alone.

It worked. "Okay." Dad gave her a few more pats of concern. "I'm always here, and Mom is, too, for you to talk to. About anything. We love you. We're on your side, Noles."

"Thanks, Dad," was the last thing Nolie remembered saying.

She must've fallen asleep like that, all curled up on her bed, hugging her pillow to her face, fully dressed. Thinking about the horrible things she'd done, taking Grandma's compass and Jessa's necklace, and how she'd dug herself into a hole she didn't know how to get out of.

Nolie woke with a jolt and the clock said eleven p.m. She had that awful fuzzy unbrushed teeth taste in her mouth. Linden was asleep in the bed across from her. She crept out into the hall to see Mom and Dad's light off under the crack of their bedroom door. So she brushed her teeth, got into pajamas, and read for hours. One of her old favorites—*Harriet the Spy*—until she finally drifted off to restless sleep again.

12

A SIMULATED WORLD

Cast lists for *Annie* were posted a couple days later. Jessa got Annie. Of course she did. Not having her crystal in hand didn't seem to ruin her good luck. You couldn't miss the news, even if Nolie didn't get to congratulate her to her face.

It seemed like Nolie and Serena were the only girls not involved with the musical.

"More time for us to work on our social studies project," Serena said. She invited Nolie over to brainstorm their ideas about home. She wanted to do something unexpected. "Let's not do it about our actual homes, which I think is kind of boring, but other places we consider like homes," she said. "Like for me, the Central Park Zoo is a place where I feel at home. I've been visiting some of the animals since they were babies. They're like the siblings I never had and never wanted." She gave a dramatic swoon, which made Nolie laugh.

On Friday Nolie stood by Serena's locker, waiting for her to pack her bag. She could feel Jessa's presence down the hall. She snuck a peek to see her and Calliope doing stupid dance moves from a video on their phones.

"Hey, no phones allowed in school," Nolie called out. Knowing she shouldn't have. It was none of her business. And she shouldn't give them the satisfaction of thinking she cared.

Calliope glowered back at her, and Jessa looked like she wanted to light Nolie on fire. Calliope slipped the phone into the pocket of her designer jean jacket. It was frayed and torn on purpose—not because she'd really worn it a million times. Unlike Serena's backpack, which was a shapeless cloth sack that she said she'd had since kindergarten. Over the years she'd covered it in colorful patches, and it was so worn in the corners that a chewed pencil stub poked through.

Nolie expected Serena's apartment to be as frayed and patched as Serena's backpack, but it was the opposite. Everything was sleek and modern with light walls and spotless wood floors, not a stray object out of place. Like an apartment you'd see in a designer magazine. Her parents were both at work, but Serena had a cool babysitter, Margot, who was in art school. She wore rings on every finger and had a nose piercing, and a flower tattoo encircled her wrist.

Serena's face lit up when she talked to Margot, chatting about their days in the quick way you have with someone you know really well. Like how Nolie and Jessa used to talk. Nolie pushed down a pang of sadness.

The kitchen was all stainless steel and soft lighting. They sat on a bench at the table and ate a snack of hummus, which Serena'd made herself, and crackers and carrots.

After telling them about a laser light art installation at a downtown gallery, which she promised to take Serena to one day after school, Margot shooed them off to do their work.

Serena's room was more like her. A faded rug on the floor, a handmade quilt draped over the arm of an easy chair, and an antique bookcase crowded with a lot of Nolie's favorite books, including *Harriet the Spy*. And, of course, her pets, Wilbur the guinea pig and Harriet the betta fish.

Serena cooed at them in their respective habitats. She dropped in some food for Harriet, who glowed bright blue and wiggled in response to Serena's finger taps on the glass bowl. Then she took out Wilbur for a cuddle. His brown and white fur was soft. Nolie laughed when he scurried up her arms, tickling her with his scratchy nails.

Above Serena's desk was a bulletin board covered in tiny pieces of paper. Nolie looked closer. Fortunes! "You collected all these? You must eat a lot of Chinese food!"

Serena laughed. "Yeah. I like the food. And the fortunes."

"So cool." Nolie leaned in to read them. She always meant to hold on to her own fortunes, especially the ones she liked. But most of the time, she threw them out or they went missing because she didn't have a special place to keep them like Serena's bulletin board. Occasionally, a random one would turn up in a drawer or pocket when she least expected it. She loved that— it was like getting the fortune all over again.

Serena had some good ones: *Look in the right places: you will find worthy offerings.*

Do not give up, the beginning is always the hardest.

Believe in your abilities, confidence will lead you on.

And some that made no sense: *A short pencil is better than a long memory any day.*

"Are these favorites?" Nolie asked. "Or every single one you've ever gotten?"

"Every one I've ever gotten. At first, my parents would give me theirs. But then I decided it only counts if I open the cookie myself."

One fortune had been ripped down the middle, and then both sides pinned back up together again: *A good home is happiness.*

Serena saw Nolie studying it. "When my parents fight . . . " she whispered. "It's like I'm waiting for them to split up. It'd be better."

Nolie didn't know what it was like to have parents

who fought so much, you'd rather they got divorced. Jessa's parents had been divorced since she was little. They still fought, but through Jessa, which was almost worse. And her dad lived across the country, so she didn't get to see him as much as she wanted.

"That's why it's good when Margot's here," Serena continued. "They can be out at work or wherever, and I don't have to deal. And when they are home, when Margot's here, I have someone else to talk to. Sometimes it sucks being an only child."

"Jessa's an only child," Nolie couldn't help but say.

"Does she hate it?" Serena asked.

"I think she kind of likes it, most of the time. She gets whatever she wants. Her parents are already divorced. They really spoil her."

Serena shrugged. "My parents aren't the spoiling type. More like the type to do whatever *they* think is best—like making me switch schools. Anyway, guess what? There's a good chance that none of this matters. I heard this really cool idea that there's a fifty-fifty possibility that we're living in a simulated world. Some scientists think that *we're* not real—this whole world isn't real. It's a made-up reality—a game that someone else is playing."

Nolie scrunched her nose. "How is that even possible?" She wasn't sure she wanted it to be possible. The idea made her anxious, not comforted, the way it did for Serena. Some things in life had to be real, even if they didn't always make you happy.

"The idea is that if you could travel at the speed of light, you could burst through the boundaries of the simulated world, into the world of the being who controls us. Something like that. But then, whoever it is playing this game, needs to change the reality they've set up for me. I'm not sure I'm happy about where they've stuck me. Child torn between fighting parents, ugh."

Nolie laughed. "Maybe that's why you want to look for places outside of home for our project? Because you don't seem to like it much here."

"Yeah. Maybe." She put on her fake blue glasses and pulled out a pencil and notepad, like it was time to get down to business. "What are your places?"

Nolie told Serena about Joey's, how the smell of rubber soles and cardboard boxes and the tattered carpet in the store felt like home to her. How it had been in her family for years, and she felt useful there, when she helped with customers or in the back office. And about Grandma's—her beach cottage and apartment. She almost included Jessa's, but didn't because she didn't think that was still true.

Serena told Nolie how Central Park was her place. How when she was younger, her nannies used to spend hours exploring the park with her on weekends, to keep her out of the house so her parents could have their peace and quiet. She loved the Ramble, the Reservoir, Belvedere Castle. "All of it, really."

"I guess that's kind of your thing," Nolie said. "The park."

"My *thing*?" Serena looked confused.

"You know, like your passion. Like what you *do*."

"Let's see," Serena said, tapping a finger to her chin. "I *do* sixth grade. I love animals, and collect fortunes and weird facts, and I explore the park. That's what I do. You?"

"Nothing," Nolie mumbled, and crossed her arms. She couldn't even claim to have a special collection—unless it was the bag of stuff from activities she'd given up on. Or the stash of things on her windowsill. She hadn't even auditioned for *Annie* or signed up to try any new activities this year. She just *was*.

"You're doing this." Serena waved her hand back and forth between them. "Becoming friends with the girl no one else wants to talk to. And you're a good listener."

Nolie liked that idea, that maybe her thing was being a good friend and listening to other people. "I thought you said you didn't want to make any friends. To prove to your mom that she was wrong for sending you to a new school?"

Serena shrugged, pushed her hair behind her ears—she had a cute enameled ladybug stud in one ear, and a bee in the other—and threw up her hands. "Sometimes you can't help it. And guess what? I have the best idea ever. Let's go to the zoo."

"Now? Or, like, this weekend?"

Serena glanced at her phone. "Now. It's still open."

Nolie wasn't used to being that spontaneous. When she and Jessa did activities, it was always planned well ahead of time. One of their moms—usually

Andie—would arrange to take them and buy tickets in advance.

"How will we get tickets?" she asked.

Serena grinned. "Wouldn't you have guessed by now? I'm a member. I don't need to buy tickets. C'mon. It's a few blocks away. You can walk home from there."

They told Margot they were going, and she said she'd get dinner started while the girls went out. Which surprised Nolie, since she assumed Margot would go with them.

But Serena knew exactly how to get there. Walking along Fifth Avenue, Serena told Nolie about the snow leopards that had been born in the zoo a few years ago, and how it was the only zoo in New York that had snow monkeys. She even did camp there in the summer and got to go behind the scenes with some of the animals, which was the best thing ever.

There was no line to get in so late in the day. At each exhibit Serena told Nolie more facts about the animals. Nolie listened and tried not to gag on the animal stench. She wondered how the animals felt. Were they happy living behind a plastic barrier that people watched them through? Did they realize they were in exhibits and not in their natural worlds?

Maybe it was kind of like they were performers on stage—like Linden. How the ballerinas create a magical world in *The Nutcracker* that you long to believe in. You can let yourself fall into the magic of it when you're in the audience. But once you go backstage, you see that none of it is real. The giant Christmas tree is flat, made of wire strung with pine needles. The bed moves across the stage on a special track. The snow that falls from above is nothing but tissue-thin bits of paper.

"Do you think they know we're watching them?" Nolie asked. "Do you think they like it?"

"I'm sure on some level," Serena said. "Have you ever come to the sea lion feedings? They totally put on a show. They're really intelligent animals, and they're trained to do flips and dives and stuff. They get rewarded for it with food. No different than dogs, I guess. The sea lions are so smart, they'd be bored if they didn't learn new stuff."

People, too, Nolie thought to herself. People needed to learn new stuff, to change the ways they did things. Sometimes.

Maybe she'd been stuck in her way with Jessa for too long. Maybe that's why things were changing now. Not just because Jessa was being mean. Maybe Nolie also needed something different. If she'd been with Jessa at the zoo, she'd never have thought about all these interesting things that came up with Serena.

On her way home, Nolie felt hope expand in her chest, like the moment when a balloon begins to fill with air.

And that night, when she opened *The Odyssey* for her homework reading, out fell a tiny rectangle of paper that had been tucked into the pages.

Nolie picked it up.

A fortune. Ha!

She unfolded it: *A new friend will help you break out of an old routine.* She'd swear it wasn't one she'd ever gotten before. A little smile crossed her face. She had a feeling she knew where it came from.

And she had just the place to keep it.

Nolie put Serena's fortune on the windowsill, along with the rest of her collection.

But while Serena's fortune was something that had been given to her, for her to keep, Grandma's compass and Jessa's necklace still needed to be returned.

Except returning them felt impossible.

The long weekend ahead was a welcome break from thinking about how to return the necklace to Jessa. Monday was Rosh Hashanah, the Jewish New Year, which meant a day off from school. But it also meant going over to Grandma's for the first time since she'd taken the compass.

13
NEW YEAR

Rosh Hashanah was Nolie's favorite Jewish holiday—a time for new beginnings, marked by apples and honey, special round challah, and the blowing of the shofar at synagogue.

That year, Rosh Hashanah was at the very end of September, which was considered late. It was a perfect crisp fall day, brilliant with sunshine and cool air. They went to family services at Temple Emanu-El, then walked back through the park to Grandma's for lunch. Aunt Eve, Uncle Matt, and the cousins, who they hadn't seen since their ruined Cousins Week, would also be there. It would be a perfect day, as long as no one noticed the missing compass.

Nolie decided she couldn't risk returning it with everyone there. Besides, she didn't have a pocket big enough to carry it, and it would look weird if she carried a bag to temple. Especially given that the security guards at the temple would need to inspect her bag.

At Grandma's, everyone greeted each other with kisses and the New Year good wishes, "Shanah tovah." Linden and Anna sat together at one end of Grandma's dining table, because they were the older sisters. And Nolie got stuck with Gabe and Eli. They'd turned nine last week, and Aunt Eve had decided they were old enough not to need her to sit between them and keep them under control. Now, apparently, it was Nolie's job.

The boys attacked the challah before Nolie could get a piece, so all that was left for her was a pile of crumbs and a hard edge of crust. They dripped honey-dipped apples on her sleeve, and she would've been soaked by water if she hadn't seen the glass tipping and saved it just in time.

"Catch this!" Eli launched a pea at Gabe, using his

spoon as a catapult, right across Nolie.

Next Gabe scooped up mashed potatoes.

"Oh, no you don't!" Nolie grabbed Gabe's wrist, squeezing tight to stop him.

"Ow, Nolie, that hurts!" Gabe screamed, drawing all the attention to her. As if it were her fault that they were about to start a full-on food fight.

If Nolie tried to defend herself and say that the boys started it, Aunt Eve would make a comment to Dad about how Nolie was supposed to be the older, responsible one.

So she kept her mouth shut and tucked her hands in her lap where she could pick at the dry skin on her thumb. She squeezed herself as small as possible. But the twins found a way to jab and elbow her, no matter what she did to try to disappear.

Linden and Anna sat at the other end of the table, too far away for Nolie to join their conversation. Their heads bent close together over a phone that Anna had snuck on to her lap. So much for them being perfect.

The adults had the usual catch-up conversation. Aunt Eve boasted about how Anna was torn between focusing on violin and riding. Gabe was a budding chess master, and Eli had discovered a talent for singing that no one ever knew he had. He'd gotten a starring role in their community theater's production of *Oliver,* and Aunt Eve and Uncle Matt had already bought out the front row for opening night. They had to save the date now.

Great. Another star in the family.

Dad let Aunt Eve finish her bragging before he got started about Linden. Marie. *The Nutcracker.* Of course, they couldn't return the favor of buying out the front row on opening night because, you know— Lincoln Center and the orchestra seats were way too expensive.

"And Linden's bat mitzvah is coming up, too?" Aunt Eve said, changing the subject. "We're all looking forward to that." She waited, expectantly, for Mom or Linden to give more information about what they were doing to celebrate. Anna had had a morning service, followed by a kiddush lunch at their temple in New Jersey and a huge black-tie party that night at an event space. Linden said that she didn't even want a party, just the lunch after the service.

"We're keeping it low-key," Mom filled in for

Linden. "Maybe a small party for her friends in the evening, but we'll keep you posted."

Aunt Eve gave her a curious look, like she couldn't understand why a girl turning thirteen wouldn't want a wedding-like celebration.

"And how about you, Nolie?" None of the other kids had been asked to speak for themselves. But now Aunt Eve was asking her directly what she had to show for herself.

Nolie shrugged and looked to Grandma.

"I hear Nolie's on her way to mastering the family business," Grandma said with an encouraging lilt. "Dad tells me what a help you are at Joey's."

Dad's face brightened. "Nolie's great with the balloon machine. The kid customers love her. She helped us sell through a few pairs last time she was in the store."

"I've always known she's got the entrepreneurial spirit," Grandma said. "Ever since you and that friend started that business together at the beach. Bracelets. Maybe we could sell some at Joey's."

"Grandma, that was so last year!" Nolie blurted out. She and Jessa had a short-lived business selling friendship bracelets at a stand they'd set up when she came to visit at Grandma's beach cottage the summer before fifth grade.

Grandma looked hurt. "Maybe you should get back to it. They were very well done, I thought. Nice color sense. I still have mine." Nolie glanced at Grandma's wrist. A threaded friendship bracelet would look totally out of place with her gold and diamond bangles. "I keep it on my bedside table."

Nolie could sense Anna and Linden smirking down the table, holding in their laughter. She studied the pattern of green and gold leaves on the china dinner plates.

"Well, thankfully Nolie's got the right touch," Grandma went on. "Someone needs to take over the business."

"I can totally see it," Linden piped up. "Cross out 'Joey's' and change it to 'Nolie's'!" But she didn't say it nicely. She said it in a way that she could barely get the words out through gasps of laughter. Anna and the twins cracked up, too. The anger and humiliation thudded in Nolie's chest.

"What's so funny?" Grandma turned to Linden. "Is there something funny about the shoe business?"

A thrill ran through Nolie at Grandma coming to her defense.

"Um, no." Linden pressed her lips together and sat up straighter in her chair.

"Ew, Nolie! Blood!" Eli screamed, pushing his chair back from the table.

She looked down at her thumb. Without even realizing, she'd ripped the dry skin. The spot that she'd picked at during temple. During this whole, stupid meal. A trickle of blood seeped down her thumb onto Grandma's lacy linen napkin.

Mom's face went from flat, trying to stay out of the banter, to alert and alarmed. She was up and at Nolie's side in an instant. "Here." She handed her a tissue. Nolie wrapped it around her thumb and pressed it to the broken skin. Her face burned with shame.

"Lenore, do you have a Band-Aid?" Mom asked.

Grandma went to the drawer in her kitchen where she kept supplies.

She ripped open the paper and peeled off the backing.

"I can do it myself, Grandma," Nolie said. But

Grandma had the Band-Aid all ready, so Nolie held up her thumb like a little girl and let her wrap it. As she leaned in to secure it, Grandma's soapy, floral scent filled Nolie's nose. It reminded her of the hours they'd spend looking through her clothes and jewelry drawers in her closet, Grandma describing all the special objects she'd collected over the years.

But that only made her think of the compass and how she'd prayed in temple that no one would discover it missing. And about Jessa and her grandma and the lucky crystal necklace.

After lunch, when everyone lounged around in Grandma's living room, Nolie crept into her bedroom. The blue-and-white flowered fabric of the headboard blended in with the wallpaper behind it and the curtains around the window, so you felt like you were in a blue-and-white flowered treasure box. The smell of her perfume was even stronger in here.

On Grandma's bedside table were framed photos: Dad and Aunt Eve as children at Joey's Shoes, the cousins at Anna's bat mitzvah, Linden and Nolie in matching dresses, a large photograph of the whole family at the beach when Grandpa Leon was still alive and Nolie was only three years old, so she didn't remember.

And, in a porcelain dish that held a few precious knickknacks, including Grandma's gold wedding band which she didn't always wear, there was the lavender and green friendship bracelet. Nolie picked it up, rubbing its silky threads between her fingertips. She couldn't remember which of them had made it—her or Jessa. It hadn't mattered then. She'd thought she and Jessa would be best friends forever, so she didn't mind if Jessa was the one who made Grandma's bracelet. If she'd known then how things would be now, she wouldn't want Jessa to have anything to do with something made for Grandma. Something special, that Grandma had kept and held on to, even now.

She wanted to slip the bracelet into her pocket. To take it away, so Grandma had no part left of her and Jessa's friendship.

But she knew Grandma. Now that she'd mentioned it at lunch, she'd look for it. And it would be one more thing that Nolie took that didn't belong to her.

She sucked in a deep breath, held it, counted to three, and let it out. She squeezed her bandaged thumb tight, wishing she could pick at the raw skin beneath. She resisted the urge and left the curl of friendship bracelet where it belonged.

She took in another deep breath, and this time she made a wish. She wished upon Grandma and all her treasures that she'd make the right choice. Do the right thing. She had to return the things she'd taken. Jessa's necklace, first.

The simplest thing would be to pull Jessa aside at the end of the day. Tell her that the necklace had fallen out of her locker (slightly glossing over the truth), and that Nolie had picked it up to return to her. Then she got scared when Jessa put the signs up and didn't know what to do.

Something like that.

But when they got home from Grandma's, and Linden was showering, Nolie went to the place on the windowsill where she kept her collection.

Jessa's crystal necklace was gone.

14

THE MISSING CRYSTAL

Nolie checked the floor under her bed and ran her fingers between her mattress and the bed frame. She peeked under the crack beneath the radiator, sneezing four quick times in a row from the dust, to make sure it hadn't fallen.

Nope. Not there.

Linden came in from the shower. She looked regal, even with her wet hair wrapped up in a towel, another towel tucked around her chest in that way that never worked for Nolie. It always slipped off when she tried to wrap herself like that.

But Nolie didn't say anything about Jessa's crystal,

even as she studied Linden. It was no mystery who'd taken the necklace. Linden was the only person it could've been.

Which meant that Linden *knew*. She must've seen all the things: Grandma's compass. Jessa's crystal. Serena's fortune. The seashell necklaces.

And while Serena's fortune was a gift, Linden would know the other things weren't. She'd know that Nolie had fished her seashell necklace out of the trash. That Nolie had taken Grandma's compass. And, of course, Jessa's crystal.

Linden knew, and hadn't said anything.

Had she already known about it when she brought it up over Taco Tuesday? And when did she take the crystal away?

It'd still been there last week—was it Friday?— when Nolie put Serena's fortune on the windowsill next to it.

So, sometime over the weekend.

But why wouldn't Linden have proclaimed her big discovery right away? Hold it over Nolie? Force her to return it to Jessa? Or even worse: What if Linden had already gone and returned it to Jessa?

Told Jessa what Nolie'd done?

Nolie watched Linden unwind the towel from her head, comb out her long brown hair, and put on her pajamas. She watched her weave her damp hair into two braids so it would be wavy the next day. She watched Linden examine her face in the mirror for barely-there pimples. She watched her go through her planner, making pencil marks to cross off her completed assignments.

But Linden didn't watch Nolie, in return. She didn't even notice Nolie watching her. It was like nothing had happened, like Linden hadn't discovered the crystal.

She supposed there was the slightest chance that it wasn't Linden.

Maybe Mom had finally decided to clean back there. But why would she have taken away the crystal and left the other things?

Nolie would have to do some snooping of her own to find out if Linden had it.

Later, after Linden fell asleep, Nolie turned on her reading flashlight. She cast the spotlight near Linden, to watch her. To make sure she was really

asleep and not faking. When she was falling asleep—
or pretending to be asleep so she could ignore Nolie—
she'd be all scrunched up in a tight ball. But now,
her arms were flung wide open, which she only did
in deep sleep. And even in sleep, Linden's eyebrows
pulled together, her arms twitched, her lips twisted
in worry—maybe about Charlotte. Or something else
altogether.

Nolie glanced toward Linden's ballet duffel,
which was wearing thin from so many years of use.
It slouched at the foot of her bed, innocently enough.
The pink embroidery gave it a cheerful appearance
that no longer matched Linden's moods.

The duffel would be one of the places she'd have
put Jessa's necklace. Or her desk drawer.

Nolie tiptoed over to Linden's desk on her side
of the room. Unlike Nolie's, it was neat with plenty
of clear space on top. Her books were stacked in a
certain order, her pencils sharpened and organized
in one container, her pens in another, all with their
matching caps.

And her planner, flipped open to the current week,
showed all her assignments with lines crossed through

the ones she'd completed. As usual, she was well on top of, if not ahead of, her work. She got it done during study halls, after school, before class or rehearsal. Nolie knew that if she'd been in Linden's place—if she were the one with the serious ballet career—she'd be staying up all night to finish her homework and get totally sleep-deprived.

Nolie didn't even need to sift through Linden's desk drawer because everything inside was as organized as the stuff on the outside. Whereas Nolie's desk drawer could hardly open because she shoved things in to hide them whenever Mom complained about her needing to be more organized.

Next, the duffel.

Nolie knelt, balancing the reading light on her lap. She grasped the zipper and started to pull, when suddenly there was movement and a snuffling noise in the bed. She sang *Simple Gifts* three times over in her head before she tried it again to make sure Linden was still sleeping. A deep snort—the kind of indelicate noise that Linden would never make if she was awake—reassured her.

This time Nolie got the zipper open on the side

WHERE YOU'VE GOT TO BE

pocket. A peek inside showed nothing but a handful of change, a few sticks of mint gum, and some Band-Aids. One of the end pockets had a wad of tissues and a keychain with a ballet slipper charm. And in the other—there it was!

Jessa's crystal necklace.

Nolie squeezed her fist around it, wanting to take scissors to that shiny necklace cord and snip it to pieces.

But it wasn't Jessa she was angry at now—it was Linden. How could she take the crystal and not even tell Nolie? What was she planning to do with it? Had she already told Jessa? Or was she taking it to school with her tomorrow—to show Jessa? To return it to her?

Or worse, maybe she would go straight to the principal, to get Nolie in trouble. There's no way she could trust Linden and Jessa not to tell anyone— everyone—that Nolie was the one who took it.

If the seventh graders knowing about how she'd thrown up on the bus was bad enough, wait until the whole school found out about this.

Nolie jumped to her feet, ready to shake Linden

awake and confront her right away.

But then, Nolie saw something else.

A piece of lavender paper in the pocket. Jessa's monogrammed lavender paper. Folded up into a small square. With Linden's name written on the outside in Jessa's bubbly handwriting.

Nolie unfolded it and shone her flashlight on the note:

Linden: I <u>KNOW</u> Nolie took my necklace. She won't admit it to me. I don't know why she did it and I don't care. I just <u>really</u> need it back. Can you pretty please try to help me find it? I bet it's in your room somwhere. Or else, I'm going to have to tell the principel. xoxJessa

Nolie's stomach turned. The humiliation stung and tears of rage pricked, but she squeezed them back.

She felt like a baby. Like Jessa was somehow beyond her now, more on Linden's level, and they were the older girls figuring out together how to handle a problem like Nolie.

She wanted to take that note and the necklace and destroy them both.

But it wouldn't help. It wouldn't take away what Nolie'd done, and that Jessa and Linden both knew about it.

She'd been caught. Plain and simple.

15
LUCKY OR NOT

Nolie woke up the next morning feeling like she'd barely slept. The last thing she wanted was to face the day. Remembering about the necklace and Jessa's note felt like a bad nightmare that she couldn't wake up from.

She decided to test Linden—like a game of chicken—to see who would bring it up first. She kept quiet all through breakfast, watching Linden, to see if she looked at Nolie any differently. But there was nothing to give her away.

Linden did her usual morning routine of stretching, rubbing cream into her cracked and callused feet, and getting dressed. She danced in front of the mirror while she brushed out her hair and pulled it into a half ponytail that she'd later twist up into a tight bun for rehearsal. A dab of lip gloss, a swipe of mascara, a pat of face powder. A last admiring look at herself. She knew she was beautiful. Lucky Linden.

"Why are you watching me like that?" Linden finally said, speaking to Nolie's reflection in the mirror.

"I'm not." Nolie turned her gaze to study her bookshelves.

"Yes, you are."

"Am not. I'm making sure I have all my books for the day."

Linden smirked. "Since when do you care about being prepared?" And she finished getting her backpack and ballet duffel ready.

Nolie watched to see if Linden realized the necklace was gone. It was in the pocket of Nolie's bag now, while she figured out what to do with it, on her own terms.

But Linden didn't check that side pocket.

Which meant it was on Nolie to bring it up.

As soon as they were out of their building onto the

street, Nolie began, "Jessa's necklace—"

"Why, Nolie? Why'd you take it?" Linden interrupted.

Nolie's cheeks grew hot, despite the cool morning air. "I—I don't know."

"Well, you've got a lot of explaining to do. Does Grandma even know you have her compass?"

"I'm just borrowing it."

"And the seashell necklaces. I threw mine out. You took it out of the trash?" Linden pressed her lips into a hard line. "Why?"

"I don't know. I felt bad."

"For me? Or for the necklace?"

"Grandma gave them special to us. Don't you think she'd be sad if she knew you threw it out?"

"She didn't know." Linden sighed. "But whatever. You're a trash collector, apparently."

The coldness of Linden's words ached like a brain freeze.

"I thought maybe you'd change your mind. Decide you'd want it someday."

"I'm too old for treasures," Linden said, a wistful look on her face. "But Jessa—that necklace means everything to her. She knows you took it. She asked me to help her get it back."

All Nolie wanted right now was to be a hermit crab. To slink out of the shell of who she was and find another shell to move into. In a totally new place where no one knew her. If she'd listened to Jessa in the first place, followed her self-improvement list, maybe she wouldn't be in this situation. Maybe a girl named Magnolia wouldn't have done any of these things.

But she couldn't go back and do it over.

And that's not what she wanted, anyway.

"So what do I do now?" Nolie asked. "Can't you tell Jessa that you found it somewhere random? Like the bathroom or gym lockers? Or something? Cover for me?"

Linden shook her head. "That's not how this is going to work." She stopped to reach into the pocket of her duffel.

But as she fished for it, Nolie smirked, pulling out the necklace from her own backpack. She dangled it in front of Linden.

"You sneak! I wasn't going to give it back to you until you promised me that you'd return it to Jessa. Yourself."

"You give it to her," Nolie said, holding the necklace out. If Linden cared so much about helping Jessa, she could return the necklace.

But Linden didn't budge. She shook her head in refusal.

The ember of anger inside Nolie that had begun to burn at the end of the summer when Linden ruined Cousins Week burst into flames now. Nolie couldn't hold it in check any longer.

"It's all your fault!" Nolie screamed, not caring who on the street overheard them. "Everything's all about you! It's like whatever I want doesn't matter. You're so perfect and you get everything you want. And you won't even help me!"

Nolie tried to shove the crystal into Linden's hands, but Linden took a step back and threw her arms up in the air to show she wanted no part in it.

"You need to do the right thing," Linden said, pointing at Nolie, a quaver in her voice. "You stole the necklace. It's your responsibility. Or Jessa's going to the principal. And I'll back her up."

She closed Nolie's hand around the necklace.

For a few seconds, they stood there—together, on

the sidewalk, surrounded by the bustle of morning commuters and parents taking kids to school.

Nolie's chest heaved. She wanted to let out more rage, but now the crystal was warm in her hand, like a living thing. Linden's hand around hers made her remember when they were little and held hands on the street, or whenever they wanted to be connected. Until, one day, Nolie didn't know exactly when, they didn't hold hands anymore. Linden stopped reaching for her.

But now, here they were. Nolie was furious at Linden, but also didn't want to say anything that would make Linden let her go. To break the connection. Because maybe *this* would be the last time Linden held her hand. You never knew when anything was going to be the last time, until later, when you realized it was.

Like the last time Nolie and Jessa had a really great sleepover—a doubleheader—last spring. They'd stayed at Jessa's apartment the first night and cooked dinner. Stuffed shells and chocolate lava cakes. They'd slept at Nolie's the next night, and ordered in pizza, and watched *Hamilton*. Linden, Nolie, and Jessa liked to do the Schuyler sisters' songs. Linden was Eliza,

Jessa was Angelica, and Nolie'd end up being Peggy. The least important one. Which was fine with her because they were having fun.

Nolie'd had no idea that would be their last sleepover. Probably their last. She couldn't imagine her and Jessa being friends like that, again. Ever.

Not after this.

Because even if she hadn't taken—well, stolen—the necklace, they were changing and growing apart. No matter how much you thought things were perfect the way they were, no matter how much you tried to hold on, things changed.

Linden pulled her hand away from Nolie. "And who says I'm so perfect? You don't know anything." She turned and hurried off toward school, leaving Nolie alone.

Nolie looked down at the crystal in her palm.

It meant nothing. It didn't bring good luck. It was just a lifeless piece of stone.

Something only had good luck, or was considered treasure, because someone gave it that value. Things only got meaning from the significance that people gave to them.

Nolie took in a few more breaths. As angry as she was at Linden for refusing to help her, she knew she was ready.

At lunchtime Nolie found Jessa by her locker, with Calliope like an evil stepsister at her side.

Nolie clutched the crystal necklace in one hand and clenched her other hand tight to keep from picking at the skin on her thumb.

"I need to talk to you. Alone," she said.

Calliope looked to Jessa for her command, her signal that she could leave.

"I'll catch up with you at our table," Jessa said, sending her away. She stood guard in front of her locker, hands on her hips. "What now?"

Nolie's shoulders relaxed as a thought occurred to her that gave her courage. She wasn't Magnolia, pretending to be someone she wasn't. She was Nolie. And it was time to live up to her name, like Serena saw it: No Lie.

"I have something to give to you. I mean—to return."

She opened her hand to reveal the crystal necklace curled inside. The lavender amethyst looked dull against her clammy skin. Jessa plucked it up and held it to the light, like she was inspecting it for damage. Against the light, in Jessa's fingers, the crystal looked magical and luminous.

"Thanks." Jessa slipped the necklace around her neck and tucked the crystal into her shirt, so she wouldn't get called out for wearing it in school. Even though everyone would be happy to know she'd gotten it back.

Jessa didn't move, just yet, to walk away from Nolie. So Nolie waited, too. To let Jessa ask her why she took it. Or to yell at her. Which she totally deserved.

Or, maybe, Jessa was waiting for Nolie to muster up an apology. Which she owed her.

So, Nolie said the two simplest words possible: "I'm sorry."

And like a miracle, like good luck was finally coming Nolie's way, Jessa's face softened.

"Me, too." It was a tiny whisper, and she didn't say what for. Whether it was for wanting to make Nolie be someone she wasn't or for changing into someone different herself. Or for everything—their whole friendship breaking apart. But it was something.

"Is that it?" Nolie asked. "You totally have the right to yell at me."

Jessa looked confused, and she opened her mouth, like she might be about to let it out. But then she gave a sad shake of her head. "I really just wanted it back, Nolie."

Nolie nodded. She still had one more question. "So, what's the reward?" She hoped that she managed to make her voice sound teasing, not pathetic.

Jessa actually laughed, and Nolie felt a huge sense of relief. And then, Jessa leaned in and hugged her. A real, tight squeeze of a hug. A hug that smelled of Andie's sugar-sweet perfume. A hug that made Nolie think she was forgiven—its own reward. And a hug that, maybe, also meant good-bye.

"Did it bring you any luck? The crystal?" Jessa asked, genuinely curious.

"Not really." Nolie shrugged. "Maybe the bad kind. Did not having it give you bad luck?"

Jessa laughed. "No. Didn't you see? I got the role of Annie!" She gave a little squeal, and Nolie felt a thrill for her. "Maybe there's no such thing as a lucky crystal, anyway."

And with that, she turned away from Nolie. Away from believing in things like lucky crystals, and toward the dining hall. To her table, her new friends.

"You did it?" Linden asked Nolie, finding her in the locker hallway at the end of the day, before she went off to ballet.

"Yup."

"Good." Linden shook her head, like she still didn't understand. "See you later."

As Linden walked off, her backpack weighing down her shoulders, her ballet duffel slung across her chest, she looked like a tiny girl who had too much to carry.

Nolie thought about what Linden had said earlier. About her not being so perfect. Nolie knew that was true. There was plenty she'd seen about Linden that was far from perfect. The times that Linden had to say no to a friend's birthday party because she had ballet class. The way her pointe shoes made her feet ache, and how her toenails bled and cracked. She pushed herself so hard to get stronger and more flexible, contorted in unreal positions on their living room floor, that she cried out in pain.

But that was all Linden's choice, wasn't it? Being a ballerina was what she wanted. The most important thing to her. But just because she wanted it, and got it, didn't mean it wasn't hard for her, too. There were things like her competitiveness with Charlotte. The girls saying mean things. The never-ending classes and rehearsals, in addition to preparing for her bat mitzvah. The pressure to get better, to perform. Nolie had none of that. Maybe Lucky Linden wasn't so lucky. Maybe Linden was right. Nolie didn't know anything.

It was supposed to be Taco Tuesday, but for some reason Linden had a late rehearsal scheduled that night. So Nolie and Dad ordered in Mr. Tang's. Dad tilted his head when Nolie asked to order her chicken and broccoli Linden's way, steamed with sauce on the side, in case she wanted leftovers. When Mom and Linden did get home, she said she wasn't hungry.

Alone in their bedroom that night, Nolie tried to talk to her.

"Jessa was really cool about it," Nolie started. "She didn't yell or anything."

"Isn't that nice." Sarcasm dripped from Linden's voice. She didn't even turn from her book to look at Nolie.

"Yeah, I guess I have to accept that we're drifting apart. Like you said."

Linden didn't answer. She barely gave an *mmm* of acknowledgment.

"How was your day?" Nolie asked.

Linden shrugged, switched off her reading light, and turned over.

Was it some sort of silent treatment, or was Linden just tired?

Either way, Nolie had an unsettled feeling deep in her stomach. The feeling that she had somehow wronged Linden, but she didn't exactly know how.

Whatever it was, it wasn't as clear as a stolen necklace. It wasn't a matter of simply returning something she'd taken.

And without knowing what it was, she had no idea how to fix it.

16

ATONEMENT

The very next day, Jessa's neon lavender "stolen" signs started to get removed from the walls at school. Nolie kept her head down, worried that everybody knew what she'd done and would be looking at her. Or that there was a punishment to come. But Jessa went back to ignoring her, as before, and no one else said anything or seemed to know about it. There was no summons from the principal's office, or anything to show that Jessa might've told anyone what Nolie had done.

But at the end of the day, just as Nolie started to breathe easier, an even bigger shock waited for her outside of school.

Mom.

Standing right by the exit doors. Nolie couldn't miss her.

Nolie's first thought was that she was there for Linden. Linden must've needed something special—a prop for rehearsal, emergency pointe shoe repair . . . who knew.

But Linden was nowhere in sight, and Mom's focus was entirely on Nolie.

"Nolie, we need to talk," Mom said, her hand clutching the shoulder strap of her workbag.

"Hi?" Nolie asked as they started walking.

Mom's eyebrows pinched together in her trademark upset face. Her eyes even looked red, like she might've been crying. For a split second, Nolie thought the worst. What if this wasn't about her? What if something had happened to someone—Grandma? Only a real emergency could bring Mom to leave work early and come to school.

"Is Grandma okay?"

Mom's face softened a bit; her shoulders relaxed. "Oh, honey. She's fine." And then she got stern again. "I think you know what this is about."

Shame gripped Nolie.

Linden. She'd gone and blabbed to Mom.

Nolie was going to kill her.

"Let's go get a milkshake," Mom suggested.

Nolie kept her forehead pressed to the window the whole taxi ride over to the Shooting Star diner. On top of her shame and anger, she also felt sorry for herself. Mom never did anything special like this with her alone. Never went out of her way to take time off work to bring Nolie somewhere, like she did with Linden. And now, here was Mom, paying her special attention, taking her for a milkshake after school. Only not as a special treat, not to be nice. But because Nolie was in trouble.

The diner manager was happy to see them. "Where've you been?" he asked. They used to go all the time for weekend breakfasts, for fresh waffles covered in whipped cream and maple syrup with strawberries and mugs of hot chocolate. Until Linden's schedule got too busy.

Mom smiled. "Nice to be here."

They settled into a two-seater window booth and ordered their shakes—coffee for Mom, half vanilla, half chocolate for Nolie—before Mom launched in to why they were there.

"Andie called me," she began, her voice careful, measured. "She told me what happened."

Nolie's stomach clenched. *Andie?* Not Linden? Which meant that Jessa had told her mom? Jessa didn't tell Andie anything. But she'd told her what Nolie'd done? Nolie squeezed her fists tight. She still had a Band-Aid on her thumb where she'd made it bleed at Rosh Hashanah. But she found a new patch of dry skin to pick at on her other thumb.

"I returned it," she said.

"I know. And Andie said Jessa's forgiven you. But that you two are drifting apart, and it's good to have some distance." Mom reached out to put her hand on Nolie's. "Honey, look at me."

Nolie realized she'd been looking everywhere but at Mom—at the dogs being walked on the street outside, at the little kids on scooters, at the way the leaves were starting to fall and stick to the sidewalks like someone'd pasted them there for decoration.

Now she looked up at Mom. The concern traced on Mom's face made her feel awful.

"Is this something you've done before?" Mom asked.

A snapshot of the things still on her windowsill lit up in Nolie's mind. The compass, the seashell necklace . . . She couldn't bring herself to admit it out loud, but inside, she knew it was stealing. Taking things that didn't belong to her. And she had to stop. But she was scared. She could promise herself it wouldn't happen again. But she also said that whenever she picked her thumb. When it got so bad that it bled, she promised herself she wouldn't do it again. But then she found a new spot to pick—like now—or she went back to the same old spot, and she could never seem to stop for good.

Mom leaned forward, her elbows on the table, waiting for Nolie to answer. But maybe Nolie's silence said it all.

"Listen," Mom continued. "I know things have been extra busy this fall. With Linden's ballet and bat mitzvah, and Dad and I working so much. I haven't even told Linden this yet, but I've made the decision to go part-time. Not right now. Not until my time with Mr. Weiler . . . is up. But at some point. Thankfully, we can afford for me to work less."

Nolie felt even guiltier, like what she'd done was so bad that Mom had made this major life decision. "Because of me?"

"Not only because of you, or Linden. This was my decision, that Dad supports me in, for myself. I want more time. I've wanted it for a while. For me, for all of us. And by staying part-time, I can always go back to more hours someday. But for now, I want to be here more. To be more present."

Nolie nodded. She didn't fully understand what it all meant, but Mom looked at peace with her decision, relieved, almost, so it must be the right thing for her. And if that meant she might have more time, every once in a while, to do something special with Nolie, well, she wouldn't complain.

"What about Linden?" she asked.

"What about her?" Mom tilted her head to the side.

"I don't know. I feel like she's angry at me or something."

Mom took a long sip of her milkshake. "That's between you and Linden. For now, just know that I'm here for you. I know it's hard sometimes to ask for help when you're in trouble. But you can always come to me."

Mom's warm eyes and soft words spread like melting butter through Nolie's insides. "Thanks, Mom," she whispered.

It helped to hear those words, to have Mom's love and support. But Mom couldn't fix everything for her. She still had things she needed to make better on her own. She had to return Grandma's compass, and she wasn't going to ask for Mom's help with that.

But there was one thing Mom could do.

After they left the diner, Nolie pulled Mom over to Ahmed's newsstand. "I need to buy something."

She scanned the rows of candy. A flash of red. She picked out a pack of cherry Life Savers, fished out a crumpled bill from her wallet, and handed it to Ahmed. He gave her back some change, which she put into her pocket.

She held out the Life Saver pack to Mom.

"Mom, will you please give these to Tabitha?"

Mom looked puzzled as she took the pack and

dropped it in her workbag. "Sure. Should I tell her they're from you?"

"That's okay," Nolie said. "I think she'll understand."

Linden carried on her silent treatment of Nolie with persistence and determination. Nothing Nolie tried—from offering to let Linden do her makeup, to getting an ice cream together, to simply trying to talk—could get her to open up.

Linden's silence lasted a whole week: the rest of the Days of Awe, the days between Rosh Hashanah and Yom Kippur, the Day of Atonement. Atonement meant apologizing for things you'd done wrong, and Nolie had plenty of forgiveness to ask for, this year.

On the morning of Yom Kippur, Linden refused to get out of bed.

"I don't care and I'm not going!" she shouted, when Mom came in to tell her she had to get dressed immediately or they were going to be late for services.

"Grandma got you girls these brand-new dresses," Mom yelled back, all out of patience. "Come on. Get up, get dressed, let's go."

"No!" Linden yelled. "You can't make me."

Mom paced outside the door to their room. Nolie was all ready for temple, in the dress that Grandma had bought. A navy dress with a collar and pearl buttons down the front. Not the style Nolie and Linden would ever choose for themselves. But Grandma still liked to dress them occasionally, and no one wanted to disappoint her.

Except for now.

"You've got to do something," Mom huffed to Dad. "I'm all out of ideas."

Dad straightened his tie and cleared his throat, like he was going to calculate his options and come up with the most logical solution. "Lindy?" he called softly as he knocked on the door.

He went in and shut the door behind him. The low murmur of voices, Linden's whiny and upset, Dad's low and calming, sounded through the door.

The tradition was for adults to fast on Yom Kippur, to cleanse themselves of wrongdoings and focus on what they could do better. Mom and Dad fasted until they went to Grandma's apartment after temple for break fast, so they were running on empty stomachs. Linden hadn't eaten yet, and Nolie'd barely eaten. So maybe they were all just hungry.

Mom kept checking her watch, like maybe the time wasn't as late as it kept showing it was. Services started in fifteen minutes. If they jumped into a taxi right now, they'd barely make it on time.

Finally Dad came out of the bedroom, followed by Linden a few minutes later. She'd put on the stiff dress from Grandma and a bit of makeup, and brushed out her hair. With her eyes and nose all red, she managed to pull off the look of a tragic heroine.

"Ready," she mumbled.

Dad gave Mom a look that Nolie knew meant "tell you later."

"You want a banana or something to eat on the way?" Dad asked Linden.

"No, I'm fasting this year." Even though she hadn't been bat mitzvahed yet, so technically she wasn't supposed to.

The service was well underway by the time they got to Temple Emanu-El. Grandma was already seated in their row, holding their seats. She gave a look of disapproval that they were late, mixed with approval for the girls wearing the dresses she'd bought for them.

Nolie had so much to atone for that year, but it wasn't always easy to focus on the service. She usually let her mind wander, taking in all the rich details of the sanctuary—the patterns of the mosaic tiles on the walls, the vibrant colors of the stained-glass windows. Not to mention that her dress pinched around the neck. She scratched at it until her skin was red.

Linden wasn't scratching at all. Maybe her neck was itchy, too, but if it was, she didn't show it. She was like a statue of a perfect girl, with her back straight, hands in her lap, hair hanging silky like a curtain, held off her face with a velvet headband.

Of course, Linden wasn't perfect. And she wasn't a statue. Her posture and her calm, even breaths—it was all part of her ballet training.

The rabbi's sermon was something about a group of people who lived on an island of diamonds, but they don't realize how valuable they are because they're everywhere, until a stranger shows up. He comes from an island of potatoes, and they each want what the other one has.

If Nolie thought hard enough, she could connect

that story to herself. To Jessa's comment about how Nolie wanted what other people had. But right now, the thought of potatoes led Nolie to crave French fries, which made her stomach growl.

As the rabbi described how they could repent for their wrongdoings, make apologies to those they'd mistreated, and ask for forgiveness, Linden's stomach let out an enormous, gurgling growl, too.

"Oops," she muttered under her breath.

"One word," Nolie whispered to her. "Chocolate babka." Grandma always made a loaf of their favorite, chocolate babka—kind of like a chocolate croissant in bread form, but even better.

"That's two words," Linden said.

Nolie rolled her eyes. But it was more than Linden had said to her in forever.

The plaintive bleats of the shofar, the ram's horn trumpet that the rabbi blew on High Holy Days, marked the end of the service. Everyone hugged and kissed and said happy holiday, "Good Yom Tov."

At Grandma's, they said the prayers, and filled their plates with food. Bagels and cream cheese, smoked salmon, sliced cantaloupe, noodle kugel, and challah. Nolie noticed that Linden took other food on her plate, but not any babka.

They usually fought over who got the bigger slice. And now, Linden was saying no?

Grandma was offended. "I'm wrapping up a piece for you to go," she said to Linden. "This is a personal insult to my baking skills, my dear." But not even that got Linden to accept a slice.

"Don't you want some?" Nolie asked as she sat next to Linden on the couch, balancing her plate on her knees, enjoying the babka melting in her mouth. She waved a piece on her fork in front of Linden's nose to tempt her to take a bite.

Linden swatted Nolie's arm away. "I have a stomachache."

And then, Gabe set down his plate on the coffee table, leaving a trail of babka crumbs behind him, and wandered over to Grandma's table of treasures. Specifically, the table with the magnifying glass and the letter opener.

The table where the compass was supposed to be.

"Hey, Grandma, where's your compass?" he called out.

Nolie cringed inside.

Linden elbowed Nolie, giving her a questioning look: *You didn't return it yet?*

Nolie gave her big, pleading eyes in return. *Please don't say anything!*

Linden got the message and shook her head, but thankfully, kept quiet.

"Goodness," Grandma said, joining Gabe at the table to inspect the spot where the compass should be. "Must've gotten misplaced somehow."

"You promised you'd give it to me! For my bar mitzvah!" Gabe wailed.

"That's three years away," Aunt Eve shushed him. "We'll find it. I'll help you look, Mom."

Nolie almost wanted to admit to it, then and there, to stop Gabe's impending tantrum, and Aunt Eve and Grandma from wasting their time looking for it.

But she couldn't own up to it in front of their whole family. She'd give the compass back to Grandma in private. The shame of Linden and Jessa and Mom and Andie knowing about the necklace was bad enough. And now, she wanted to shrivel up and disappear, as Aunt Eve and Grandma spent a good ten minutes scanning every surface of the living room, of her bedroom, for the missing compass.

At least it gave Linden something to say to Nolie at home that night.

"You're in so much trouble," she said, shaking her head. "Didn't you learn your lesson with Jessa's necklace?"

It was a relief to have Linden speaking to her again, even if she had nothing nice to say.

"I'm not in trouble," Nolie protested. "Unless you tell on me."

"If you don't tell Grandma and return it, I will," Linden threatened.

Nolie clenched her jaw. Why did Linden think she was the police?

"It's none of your business," she said. "And besides, I have a plan."

Linden scoffed. "I'll believe it when I see it. I'm giving you until this weekend. And yeah, it is my business. If it wasn't for me helping with Jessa, you'd probably be expelled for stealing. You should thank me."

"Is that why you didn't want to go today? Because of me?"

"Nolie, you are so self-centered. It's not all about you, okay?"

"Then what is it about?"

"Nothing at all." Linden gave a sly smile. "And everything. Wouldn't you like to know."

Infuriating. Nolie wanted to throw something at her. She grabbed her pillow and before she could stop herself, she crossed the space between their beds and whacked Linden with the pillow. Right in the head.

"What?!" Linden put up her arms protectively. "What the heck?" She looked at Nolie in shock.

Nolie gave her another whack. And now Linden lunged for her, pushed Nolie to her bed, and took her own pillow to smother Nolie's face.

"Eeek!" Nolie cried, kicking her legs.

Next thing she knew, they were tussling and scrambling and wrestling each other, getting in pillow whacks when they could, like they did when they were little. It had been so long since they'd had a pillow fight. Nolie reveled in the rush of it. But then her head banged into the wall and she screamed and her leg jerked and kicked Linden hard in the stomach, and she screamed, too.

And then the door opened, and Mom said sternly, "What's all this noise? Is everyone okay?"

Their hair was tangled and their cheeks red and yet there was a glimmer in both their eyes.

They looked at each other and smiled. "All good," Linden said. "We were just having fun."

That answer meant everything. It made Nolie feel like she'd been forgiven for whatever Linden had been upset with her over—if it had even been about her in the first place.

But after Mom closed the door, Linden's face went cold again.

"Remember. By this weekend. Or I'm telling."

17

CAPTURED IN THE CASTLE

Nolie came up with a plan to return the compass two days later. On Friday, before Linden's deadline.

Serena had suggested they go to Belvedere Castle for their home project. Nolie decided to bring Grandma's compass, so she could feel like a real-life explorer. One chance to venture with it in the outside world before she gave it back. And then she'd go straight to Grandma's after, to return it. Admit what she'd done. Her insides twisted about telling Grandma. How she'd react. About the compass going to Gabe for his bar mitzvah, not to her. But it had to be done.

The imposing stone castle was in the middle of

Central Park. No royalty lived there, of course, but you could climb the steps to the terrace at the very top and look out over Turtle Pond and the open-air theater where they performed Shakespeare in the summer.

Nolie and Serena stopped for crêpes after school, so it was later in the afternoon and not too crowded by the time they got to the castle. The sky was a dull gray that felt like rain, and the humidity made you want to take your sweatshirt off. Then the breeze would rise, and you'd get a chill and put it back on again.

"Why does it feel like home to you?" Nolie asked as they approached the castle. "Does it make you feel like you're a princess or something?"

She half expected Serena to laugh, but she didn't. "Kind of, yeah," she said. "That's the whole point. How many places can you go that spark your imagination this way?"

Nolie couldn't remember the last time she'd gone anywhere to spark her imagination. But she and Jessa used to spend hours playing in the park, climbing trees and rocks, making up games.

They walked up the steps into the echoing stone

space of the visitors' center. "*Belvedere* has always sounded so fancy to me," Nolie said.

"It means 'beautiful view' in Italian."

The voices of kids above bounced off the stone walls of the tower that led to the observation deck; they waited until the kids came clattering down before entering the tower to climb the stairs.

"Hey, look what I brought." Nolie pulled the compass out of her backpack to show Serena.

"So cool!"

She let Serena hold the compass. She examined it in detail, from the design engraved on the back to the scratchy glass on the front. "Is this real?"

"Yeah," Nolie said. "Antique. It belonged to my great-great-grandfather."

Serena held the compass as she led Nolie up the narrow, twisting staircase of the tower. She narrated their journey in a quiet voice: "The two intrepid explorers ascended the stone stairs. Step by step, around and around they went. Until they got dizzy. From the winding stairs, and from anticipation and fear. What would they see, what would they find . . . "

Nolie was out of breath by the time they reached

the top. They stepped out onto the terrace, and the view *was* beautiful. The quilt of trees in the park blazed in shades of yellow and red and orange.

There were only a few other people, and they found a good spot to take in the view. Serena took pictures on her phone and continued to narrate the story of them as explorers who'd ended up in a medieval magical kingdom. "The explorers had reached the top of the castle. For now, they were safe. Away from the dragons who would destroy them with their fire. Away from the unicorns who'd been poisoned by the green waters of the pond below . . . "

The setting sun cast a golden glow on everything. More tourists trickled in behind them, and then out again. Finally, the last visitors left. They were alone.

Time ticked by, but they were too deep into the story. Nolie added parts, too. She held up her compass and guided Serena to escape the next dragon that was coming to attack them.

Until the sun sank even lower and the air grew heavier and a lightning bolt flashed, followed by a rumble of thunder.

"Hurry!" Serena shouted. "The explorers need

to get inside before the skies let loose their rage and wrath!"

The first drops fell as they turned to run. Nolie took an extra-large step to make it inside but slipped on the wet stone. She put out her hands to break her fall. Grandma's compass flew out of her hand and landed with a sickening *crack*.

Nolie gasped.

Serena stopped and wheeled around. Her face dropped when she realized what'd happened. "Oh, no! The compass was broken. All was lost. . . ."

Nolie was no longer in the mood for Serena's story.

This was too real.

The heels of her palms were scraped and dirty. But worse, the glass of the compass was shattered. Tiny veins and cracks etched across the surface. Nolie picked it up gingerly. The top of the case hung loose, the hinge broken. The arrow, which always pointed true north, now swung wildly, mirroring the panic in her chest.

"Is it ruined?" Serena looked over her shoulder.

Nolie couldn't answer. She wanted to cry. She shook her head and rubbed her face into her arm.

She wrapped the compass in her sweatshirt to keep it from breaking more, and stuffed it into her backpack. How could she return it to Grandma now, like this?

"I'm sorry," Serena said. "I'm sure we can find a place to fix it."

Not true. Grandma was the one who'd know where to fix it.

At least Serena didn't ask her more questions, like whether it was valuable or if her grandma would be mad. Because Nolie couldn't answer. She couldn't say anything. All she wanted was to get home.

But when they reached the visitor's center on the ground floor, it seemed darker and emptier than before.

It wasn't just that the sky was thick with storm clouds, and that the lights were off, and the person who worked behind the desk was gone.

It was dark because the entrance door was closed.

"Wha-at!?" Serena pulled at the handle. The heavy wooden door wouldn't budge.

It wasn't just closed.

It was locked.

Serena pulled and pounded on the door, as if

that would make a difference. The sound bounced back at them, hollow and hopeless.

"Well, this is crazy." Serena's eyes grew wide. But she didn't seem upset. Kind of exhilarated.

Nolie's panic grew. "We're locked in?" She tried to keep the quaver from her voice, but a squeak crept in.

Serena, on the other hand, launched into action, like she'd been preparing for this kind of situation her whole life. She read the signs—"Oh, see here, it says the castle closes at five p.m. And it's already five-ten. They must not have realized we were still up there"— and made calls on her phone. Neither of her parents or Margot answered.

Nolie tried her parents, and Grandma, and even Linden, but her phone wasn't getting reception. And when she tried with Serena's phone, they didn't answer, probably because they didn't recognize the number.

"Guess we'll have to wait for someone to rescue us," Serena said cheerfully. "Maybe we'll have to spend the night!"

Nolie groaned. This couldn't be happening. Someone would get their messages or answer their calls. They'd dial nine-one-one. They were going to be rescued. Any minute now.

Her chest and throat felt tight, like she couldn't breathe. What if there was no ventilation, and they suffocated? They had no food, hardly any water. And yet, she wanted to be brave. She didn't want Serena to know how worried she was.

"Oh, look, here's the number for the parks department." Serena dialed the phone number on the bottom of the sign. And her face fell a bit when she began speaking. "Hi, um, my friend and I—we kind of got locked in Belvedere Castle. Yeah. In Central Park. Yeah, we'll be here. Sure. Thanks."

With every word Serena spoke, Nolie felt relief, even though Serena seemed disappointed that help was on the way. "Ten minutes," she said. "We can sit tight. Continue our story?"

Nolie agreed. Because for the last ten minutes, knowing they'd be rescued, she could use the distraction. Maybe even enjoy it.

"So, the explorers had come to the end of their journey," Serena said. "They couldn't go it alone, now that the magic compass had shattered. . . . "

That brought Nolie back to reality. She could've enjoyed the adventure, if it weren't for the horrible fact of the broken compass.

The parks department worker who finally unlocked the door for them, however many minutes later, didn't seem happy to have been called out in the rain. But when he saw they were just kids, he got concerned.

"Maybe I should call the police to assist you," he said, hand on his radio, water dripping from his poncho.

"Oh, no, we're fine," Serena said in her confident way. "My babysitter—she's over there. Waiting for us." She waved at some random woman.

The guy squinted in the direction she was waving, through the rain, where people walked briskly, hunched under umbrellas. And he gestured for them to go ahead, because he didn't really want to be bothered to radio the police and wait in the soaking rain.

Serena grabbed Nolie's arm, and they ran.

The rain came down harder now. Grandma's building was just across from the nearest entrance to the park.

Nolie didn't necessarily want to bring Serena with

her. She had something very important to do. To confess about taking the compass. And now, *breaking* it.

But Serena was her partner in crime. She couldn't abandon her in the stormy park. They were in this together.

"C'mon," Nolie said. "To my grandma's."

18

LIGHT THE CANDLES

It turned out they weren't the only ones who sought refuge at Grandma's.

They took off their wet shoes and dropped their wet backpacks on a towel by the front door. Nolie introduced Grandma and Serena. Then, she stepped into Grandma's living room to discover they weren't alone.

Linden was curled up on Grandma's coziest chair, wrapped in the beige wool blanket Grandma used when she wasn't feeling well, sipping from a mug. Her hair was still slicked back in her ballerina bun, also wet, with some pieces coming loose in front like she too had walked through the rain to get there.

Wasn't she supposed to be at rehearsal? A gray

sweatsuit that looked more like Grandma's clothes than Linden's peeked out from underneath the blanket.

The confused look on Linden's face reflected Nolie's.

"What are you doing here?" they both asked at the same time.

"We got stuck," Serena said, before Nolie could tell her not to say anything. "Inside the castle."

This only made Grandma and Linden more confused.

"Belvedere Castle," Serena said, like that cleared things up.

"What?" Linden asked.

"You know, in Central Park. We went there for a project we're doing for social studies," Nolie said.

"And we got locked in!" Serena offered.

"But then we called and got out, obviously, and now we're here and everything's fine," Nolie said, to reassure them that they were okay. Because the last thing Nolie wanted was to cause more trouble.

"Clearly," Grandma said, not even a hint of worry crossing her face. Unlike Mom, if she'd found out what'd happened. On the contrary, Grandma seemed proud that Nolie had done this daring thing. "Sounds like quite the adventure."

"It was." Serena beamed, and curled her fingers around the mug Grandma offered to her.

Nolie took a sip from hers and let the warmth of hot cocoa soothe her insides. "Aren't you supposed to be at ballet?"

Linden gave a look to Grandma. The look that Linden and Anna shared with Grandma as the older cousins/sisters—the privileged ones. It meant, *Do I really have to include her?*

But Nolie was tired of being left out, left behind. By the way Jessa was changing, and Linden had changed, and by how they were moving on from her.

"What is it?" she asked. "You okay?" In her gentlest voice. So Linden would understand that she could let Nolie in. That even though Nolie was younger, she could handle Linden's troubles and be there for her, too.

Grandma gave Linden a nudge. "It's your story to share, Linden." Which really meant, *Go ahead and tell Nolie, and I'm not going to do it for you.*

"It's nothing," Linden said. She glared at Nolie

over the top of her mug. "Well, not nothing. But you swear—both of you"— she looked at Serena, too— "please don't tell anyone."

They nodded.

"I threw up today. At ballet."

Nolie let out a breath she didn't know she was holding. She didn't know what awful thing she'd been expecting Linden to tell her. But throwing up just meant she was sick, right? Unless it'd happened in a totally embarrassing way. Which Nolie could certainly empathize with.

A look of understanding flickered across Nolie's face.

"Yup," Linden shook her head. "Totally puked in front of everyone and it got all over me. And even on Milo! My prince. Charlotte—of all people—started laughing and couldn't stop. I mean . . . I didn't know what to do. I just burst into tears and went to the bathroom, and I was a total mess, so I grabbed my stuff and I ran. It was raining, and Grandma's is closer. So here I am."

"Are you okay?" Nolie asked. "Is it a stomach virus or something?"

Linden shrugged. "No, I don't have a fever or feel sick. I was so hungry after school, I had a soda and ate a slice and a half of pizza before rehearsal. I think I was just kind of . . . nervous."

"My sister's starring in *The Nutcracker* this year," Nolie filled in Serena, who probably knew already.

"*Was* starring." Linden's face looked grim.

"*Is!*" Nolie and Grandma said at the same time.

But Linden looked on the verge of tears. "Whatever, Noles. If you're so into it, you step in for me. I'm done."

As if Nolie could step in for Linden.

"Really? You're going to let a thing like that stop you?" Serena spoke, surprising everyone.

"It's not just that," Linden said. "I mean, yeah, it was totally humiliating. But it's also, the whole thing is really hard. I don't know if I can do it."

"It's a lot." Grandma shook her head. "A lot of pressure for kids your age."

"And it doesn't help that Charlotte has totally turned on me. I mean, when someone you thought was your best friend becomes mean—" Linden blurted out. And then she clamped her hand over her mouth, like she realized she'd said too much. Or she realized, maybe, that it was like what'd happened to Nolie, with Jessa.

"Who's Charlotte?" Serena asked.

"My ballet ex-best friend," Linden said.

"The other Marie," Nolie explained.

"It's just hard," Linden said. "I'm always so tired. The teachers, they're really understanding, and they try not to put the pressure on us. But it's a huge deal. And we all feel it."

"Sometimes you need to step away, take a short break," Grandma said. "And then when you're ready, you'll go back and face it. You've worked too hard for this to give it up."

Tears streamed down Linden's face, and Grandma pulled her into a hug, and Nolie felt tears in her eyes, too. But this moment was about Linden, now. It wasn't about Nolie. And for once, it wasn't about serving Linden, bowing down to her needs, like when they had to cut short Cousins Week. Now, it was about *helping* Linden.

✳ ✳ ✳

"You're so lucky to have a grandma like that," Serena whispered to Nolie later as they said good-bye when Margot got there to pick her up.

Nolie smiled. She knew she was. Sometimes, luck came in the form of people, not objects.

Mom arrived straight from work and fussed over Linden, taking her temperature which was still totally normal. It was good, in a way, because it took the attention away from Nolie for almost getting locked in a building in Central Park overnight.

But there was still something pressing on Nolie. Something she really had to do. While Mom was inspecting Linden for any signs of illness, Nolie told Grandma she had something she needed her help with.

"Can I show you in your room?" Nolie asked.

Nolie pulled out the sweatshirt from her backpack and unwrapped it on Grandma's bed to reveal the broken compass.

Grandma gasped. And covered her mouth with her hand. Nolie had finally gone and done something that shocked even Grandma.

"But how—Eve and I looked everywhere for it! I was

going crazy, wondering where it'd gone. And you . . . "

Nolie looked down at the floor. She couldn't bear to see the disappointment on Grandma's face.

"What exactly happened?" An unfamiliar quaver in Grandma's voice. She didn't sound like the always calm Grandma, the one who offered steadiness and reassurance. Who always said you couldn't take your things with you to the grave, and gave away treasured objects like they were meant to be passed on to others, not to be hoarded for herself. This grandma, now, held the broken compass in her hands like it was a baby bird with a broken wing.

"I'm so sorry, Grandma," Nolie said, still looking away. "I took it—kind of to borrow it. Even though I know it was wrong to do without asking. And I was bringing it back to you, today, but then, Serena and I were pretending . . . in the castle. And I slipped and . . . I know how important it is to you, and about giving it to Gabe, and I'm so, so sorry," Nolie mumbled into her chest.

"Look at me, Nolie," Grandma commanded. Nolie could barely look up, she was so filled with shame. Grandma set the compass down on her dresser. "You're right. The compass is important. But it's just a thing. I can get it fixed. Believe me, I know where to take it."

Grandma pulled her into a hug, and now it was Nolie's turn to let her tears flow. The relief from the pressure of it all. Everything that was changing and breaking apart.

"But I'm not pleased that you took the compass without telling me. If you'd asked to borrow it, I'd have let you. You know that. There was no need to take it. That's something else."

As she stroked Nolie's head, soothing her, the light in the room changed. Mom and Linden were standing in the doorway. Watching everything.

"Is this about the compass?" Linden asked.

Grandma nodded, and Nolie's face burned.

"The compass?" Mom echoed.

"Nolie, you can explain," Grandma prompted her. The same way she'd prompted Linden to tell about throwing up.

So Nolie did. She told it all. How she'd found Linden's seashell necklace and taken it (Linden rolled her eyes), and then the compass, and Tabitha's Life Savers, and Jessa's crystal, and she took these things and she didn't know why, but she knew it was wrong, and she had to stop. She even told them how she'd broken the compass, and how awful it was.

"My girls," Mom said, pulling them to her side, one under each arm. "What a week it's been."

It was Friday, after all. Shabbat. The day of rest. They didn't always observe Shabbat at home, just the four of them, but Grandma made sure to have a challah and a glass of wine and lit the candles every week, even when she was alone.

Mom called to tell Dad to meet them there after work for an impromptu Shabbat dinner. Grandma ordered in a roasted chicken and cooked up some mashed potatoes and string beans. She said the prayers as she lit the Shabbat candles—the tall white pillars in the tarnished silver candlesticks that had been passed down in her family for generations. From the old country, she always said. Dad said the prayer over the wine.

And Nolie got to do her favorite part—the prayer over the challah: *"Baruch atah Adonai Eloheinu melech ha'olam hamotzi lechem min ha'aretz. . . ."* She embraced the idea of blessing God for giving them bread—because that delicious, pillowy challah was by far the best part of Shabbat.

At that moment, surrounded by her family in the light of the candles with delicious food spread before them on the table, Nolie was just where she wanted to be. Some things might break, but other things, or even the broken things, came together in new ways.

When Grandma said good-bye, she pulled them each close.

"Love you, see you soon," Nolie whispered to her.

"Love you more, see you soonest," Grandma said back.

The smell of Grandma's perfume lingered in their bedroom when they got home that night. From her gray sweatsuit, which Linden had draped over the foot of her bed, like a comforting blanket.

They'd already showered and were ready for bed. But it was hard to go straight to sleep. Even for Linden. They were both restless and edgy.

"Let's go somewhere," Linden said.

It wasn't that late, and the rain had stopped.

"Where?" Nolie asked, weary. She'd had enough adventure for one day.

"Where would Mom and Dad let us?"

"Ice cream?" Nolie suggested. There was an ice cream place down the block and across the street, which was close enough that their parents would let them go alone at night.

They threw on leggings and sweatshirts.

"And one more thing," Linden said. She reached to the windowsill, behind Nolie's headboard, and pulled out the seashell necklaces. She didn't even have to say anything. They both slipped the cords on, and smiled.

Linden told Mom they were going to get ice cream.

Mom looked up from the book she was reading, then checked her watch. "Are you sure? You don't feel sick at all? You want me or Dad to go with you?"

"C'mon, I'm fine. Special sister time," Linden said, in a pleading, upbeat voice.

Mom softened. She could never resist a show of sisterly bonding. "Okay," she said. "Make sure you have your phones and be back within a half hour."

Downstairs in the lobby, José held the door open for them. "Have fun!"

"Thanks," they said with a wave.

Nolie ordered mint chocolate chip in a cone, and Linden got cookie dough.

"Crazy day, huh," Linden said, in between bites.

"Yeah," Nolie said, crunching down on a chip. She felt sophisticated out alone with her sister at this hour, when the sidewalks were mostly full of adults going out to bars and restaurants. Some older teenagers. But not so many kids her age, alone. Or just with their sister. In the dark.

"It's weird," Linden said. "I mean, I feel totally fine now. I just don't know how I'm going to go back," Linden sighed. "I guess it's payback for when I told my class about you."

Nolie shrugged. "You got it worse. But you know, Grandma's right. You'll go back in and face it."

"I guess," Linden said. "But truth is, I don't know if I want to face it. To be a ballerina. I love dancing. It's the only time I feel free. It makes me happy. But performing is different. You spend all this time trying to make it look effortless and perfect. When behind the scenes, it's not like that."

Nolie nodded. It made her think of Jessa, wanting

to appear a certain way for the world. And of Serena's fake glasses. How Nolie'd tried them on, to see how they felt. But as soon as she'd put them on, she knew they weren't right for her.

Maybe that's how you figured out life—one step at a time. By trying on and doing different things. Some things worked, and some didn't, and eventually, you'd figure it out.

"You've got this," Nolie said. "If I could face Jessa, you can face Charlotte."

Linden laughed. "Yeah, we're strong like that." She took in a deep breath. "You know, I was thinking. I'm going to tell Charlotte why that comment bothered me so much. About me looking too Jewish. She needs to know why I found that so hurtful."

Nolie nodded. "Good idea." If people just said how they really felt about things more often, it would solve a lot of problems.

As they ate their ice creams, the girls walked west all the way to Riverside Park, along the Hudson River. They didn't usually go into the park at night, but neither of them stopped.

They crossed the promenade to the iron fence

along the river and leaned against the rail, their backs to the few people who were running and cycling at this time of night. Facing toward the wide ribbon of river, the whoosh of the cars speeding by on the parkway.

The river was alive. Not like the ocean, where Grandma's beach cottage was. The ocean waves curved and crashed in toward you when you stood on shore. Like the ocean was beckoning, asking you to come and join it. Nolie closed her eyes and imagined herself in the water. Helpless, giving in to the current, being pulled wherever it would take her.

But that's not what she wanted. She didn't want to be pulled along like a piece of driftwood. She wanted to make her own way through the water.

She opened her eyes to the sight of Linden breaking off pieces of her ice cream cone and crumbling them into the river.

"What are you doing?" Nolie asked, puzzled.

"Tashlich," Linden said. "My Hebrew tutor told me about it. It's a tradition, on Rosh Hashanah, to cast away your sins into a body of water. You're supposed to use bread to represent the sins you're casting off, but I figure ice cream cone crumbs are close enough. It sounded like a cool thing to do." Linden crumbled the last bits of her cone into the river below.

Nolie only had the bottom third left of her cone. The last bite was the best part of an ice cream cone, in her opinion, when there was a burst of ice cream flavor in your mouth as you crunched down that very last bit.

But if anyone needed to cast off sins, it was her. So she took her last piece of cone and crumbled it into the river, like Linden.

"There," Nolie said, not sure that anything was different. That she'd really done anything.

But maybe, just maybe, there was something. It was in how she felt closer to Linden, in a way she hadn't since before the summer. In how she'd made a new friend. And how she was getting ever nearer to figuring out where and what and who she was meant to be.

Linden wrapped her arm around Nolie, huddling tight against the chill of their ice creams and the night air. Nolie put her arm around Linden, and leaned her head against her sister's. Sisters, together, even as they go their separate ways.